JUST ONE KISS

THE FIRST LOVE SERIES

MAGGIE DALLEN

ONE

Mara

IS it super petty to hold a grudge for a decade?

Possibly.

Okay, *probably*.

But in my defense, I'm nothing if not constant. I can be depended on to hold a grudge—*and* to be on time for my shift.

I shield my eyes from the sun's glare as I glance up at the giant clock hanging over the entrance to the Lakeview Country Club's main office.

He's late. Again.

Just as the minute hand hits five after the hour, Ryan comes strolling out from the clubhouse wearing sunglasses, with his dark hair slightly mussed like he's just rolled out of bed. I blow my whistle to get his attention and he smiles. The idiot *smiles*, like I'm greeting him with that whistle and not publicly reprimanding him for being late.

He's already in his swim trunks and ready to go, but that doesn't change the fact that he's late. It also doesn't change the fact that the mere sight of my lifelong nemesis automatically makes my blood pressure skyrocket. When he strides straight toward me with that cocky grin every muscle in my body tenses.

Ryan Hunter, ladies and gentlemen. The guy who's been annoying the crap out of me since kindergarten.

I point to an imaginary watch on my arm, but he doesn't make a single attempt to pick up the pace. He's ambling over toward me, taking the long way around the giant pool like he's having a casual stroll on a Sunday afternoon.

I blow the whistle again, mainly because it's stress relief. It's the only outlet I have for this boiling rage that I've never been able to shake.

He gives me a smile and a salute, and I wish I could give him the finger in response. But considering there are currently five children under the age of ten in my shallow area of the pool, I refrain.

"You're late," I say instead as he walks toward me.

"By five minutes," he says.

"Late is late."

He stops short when he reaches the lifeguard stand. "You're so hot when you nag."

"It's not nagging if I'm your boss." I climb down off the stand. "It's your manager reminding you of the rules for the millionth time this summer."

Before he can respond, the little girls in the pool are shouting for Ryan's attention. "Watch me, Ryan, I can do a backflip!" That comes from Evie May, a girl whose mom is on the country club board.

"Nice work," Ryan says, squatting down by the pool's edge to give her a fist bump.

Evie grins like she's just won the lottery, because even grade school girls have a crush on Ryan. I can't entirely blame them since they don't know his personality. All they see is the tall, tanned lifeguard with a chiseled jaw, broad shoulders, a six-pack, and bright blue eyes.

So you know, I get that they have a crush. It's my fellow female staff members' crushes that make me wonder about their sanity. Because they've *met* the guy.

I sigh, hands on hips as I wait for him to stand up, turn around, and at least acknowledge the fact that he's wrong. Just once, I'd love to hear the words, *you're right, I'm wrong* coming from his smug, smirky mouth. It'll never happen. But a girl can dream, right?

I'd sell my soul for an *I'm sorry* from this guy, but after ten years of waiting for an apology, I'm not holding my breath.

I tap my bare foot on the water-drenched edge of the pool. We have to do this whole lifeguard checklist routine when he takes over for his shift. I'm not off-duty entirely—I still have work to do in the office. Part of the glories of being assistant manager means I get to do loads of paperwork. But I've been out here baking in the sun for the past four hours. I'm hot and I'm hungry and...yeah, okay, maybe I'm a little hangry because my irritation is way more extreme than it should be.

But still. Ryan knows I've been waiting for relief and he's taking his sweet time about it on purpose just to annoy me, I know it.

My foot's splashing in a little puddle, making an obnoxious slapping sound that he can't miss. He knows I'm standing right there. He knows I'm waiting. He knows this, and yet he takes his sweet time talking to Evie and her friends like he's got nothing better to do.

Which, by extension, is basically saying that *I've* got nothing better to do than wait around for him to pay attention to me.

"How's your backstroke coming along?" he asks Evie's friend. "Have you been practicing?"

That's it. I'm done playing nice. I lift the whistle that's hanging around my neck and blow as hard as I can right behind him.

Phwwwwwwhht!

The girls in the pool wince at the loud, long whistle blast. But Ryan? He doesn't even flinch.

He stands up slowly. Too slowly. And turns to face me with that smirk I despise. "If you want my attention, Sunshine, all you have to do is ask."

The girls in the pool giggle at his low, too-cool-for-school drawl.

Me? I sneer at the mention of my childhood nickname. Not for the first time, I wish pink had been my favorite color as a kid. Or purple. Or blue. Basically, any other color of the rainbow because then I wouldn't have gotten stuck with the Sunshine nickname.

Not that anyone calls me that anymore. I am so not a *Sunshine* kind of girl. I'm a whistle-blowing, clipboard-carrying, straight-A student, senior-class-president kind of girl. But that's why it's even worse when Ryan calls me that. It's clearly a joke at my expense.

Those are the only kinds of jokes Ryan knows how to make.

"So." He flashes me a grin that I despise. "Did you want to go through the checklist or did you just want to hang out with me for a while?"

I mutter under my breath as I snatch up the clipboard

and go through the list, each of us signing off. I walk away as quickly as I can.

As if it's not bad enough that Ryan and I are in all the same classes, having to work together every day of the summer has been torture. But the summer's almost over, and the pool will be closing for the season in a week, and after one last year of high school together, he'll be out of my hair for good.

I slow my pace as I reach the lifeguard station and try to imagine a world in which I don't see Ryan every single day. A world where I'm not constantly competing with him.

Sounds like heaven.

In reality, it's college. But college requires money, which means hustling my butt off this year and going after every scholarship opportunity I can find. Which means...

I sigh as I sink down into the faded old office chair behind the desk. Which means, keeping my head in the game. Now is not the time to take my eyes off the prize.

Hours pass by in a blur of boring admin work, answering the phone and doing the requisite inventory for the safety equipment and first-aid kits. I'm just about done with my shift's paperwork and have long since devoured the lunch I brought from home when my phone buzzes with a text. It's my best friend Celia, who's a member of this club, along with most of our classmates.

Celia: Heads up. Crush alert.

I straighten in my seat, my heart leaping with excitement. Ben is here? Like me, Ben is not a member here. He, like me, only goes to Lakeview High thanks to scholarships and hard work. He's my people.

He's also my crush. He just doesn't know it.

Me: Where? How? Why?

I hit send before I can add any more questions. She knows what I mean. Ben's not a member, so of all the fellow Lakeview High students I'd been seeing hanging out at the club over the summer—he was not one.

Celia: He's here with Elijah.

Ah. See? Now that makes sense. Elijah's parents are loaded and I've seen him hanging out at this club over the summer enough to know that he doesn't have a summer job.

A lot of Lakeview High students don't. Of those who do, most seem to be in it for college application reasons or because their parents insist on developing a work ethic. Like Ryan, for instance. It's obvious he doesn't actually need the money. If he did, he wouldn't slack off all the time.

I pull up Ben's names in my texts and start to text him that he should swing by the lifeguard station. This is not me hitting on my crush. We legitimately have business to discuss. We're both on student council and we have a lot of planning to do before school starts up in a few weeks.

"Don't bother." My BFF's voice comes from the open doorway and I let out a little squeak at the unexpected interruption.

Celia's grin is unapologetic, and she looks cuter than cute as she leans against the doorframe in her tennis garb, her long light-brown brown hair pulled back in a low pony-tail with a few strands falling around her face, that only help to accentuate her heart-shaped face and wide, dark eyes.

If she wasn't so petite, she'd look like a supermodel with her toned thighs and the adorable little sporty outfit.

She nods toward my phone. "I told Ben you're in here. He's gonna swing by when you're getting off your shift."

I sink back into my seat. "You are the best."

Her gaze is roaming over me and her brows hitch up. "You might want to freshen up."

"You think?" I'm covered in sweat and greasy sunscreen, my blonde hair pulled back in a tight bun. I didn't exactly dress to impress this morning. Mainly I dressed to survive the heat. Which means I'm sporting a one-piece swimsuit and some short-shorts.

"I'd take a shower," she says as she continues her assessment. "But keep the outfit."

I laugh. "You think this pilly old swimsuit is that hot, huh?"

"Sweetie, we need him to see that you're female, so yeah. A swimsuit will do it."

She laughs and ducks when I toss a pen in her direction. "You're insane," I say. She's also all talk. She's outgoing and sweet as can be, but when it comes to *her* crush?

Let's just say, she's not exactly strutting her stuff.

She heads toward me and shoos me out of the chair. "Go. Rinse off. I can man the fort here for a little while."

I arch my brows. Not that I don't think she can handle answering the phone or slapping a Band-Aid on the occasional injured child—the lifeguard station also doubles as the First-Aid Station—but because she doesn't actually work here.

A fact she never seems to remember.

"I'll get in trouble," I say.

She scoffs, already sliding into the seat I'd vacated. "Please. No one is going to bust me for sitting here."

She doesn't specifically mention the fact that her parents are wealthy and influential, and that they basically own this club. She doesn't have to. We both know it.

I'm already backing up toward the door, grabbing my

gym back with extra clothes while I'm at it. "If you're sure..."

"I can handle a few boo boos," she says.

Her tone is so sure, so dismissive... I can't help myself. I lean back into the room, and ask, "What if Heath is the one with a boo boo?"

It's a low blow, and I know it.

She purses her lips in a scowl that makes me laugh as I run away before she can throw something at me.

My bestie is adorable and outgoing and bubbly and kind and pretty. But when the guy she's been crushing on since second grade comes within two feet of her?

She's incapable of speech. Or flirting. Or really anything other than blushing. The other day, Heath came to the pool to give Ryan a ride, and Celia dove into the men's locker room to avoid him.

I shouldn't use this against her, but sometimes it's just too easy.

One shower later, and I'm feeling like a human again. I'm mentally tallying all the topics I'd like to discuss with Ben—including, but not limited to, how I'd like him to be my boyfriend.

Kidding, kidding. I'm not gonna bring that up. But I am hoping now that we're working so closely together he'll start to see what a good fit we are on his own.

I glance down at the sundress, running fingers through my still-damp hair.

It's not like he hasn't seen me before—we had several classes together last year, and we even ate lunch together occasionally—so I don't know what I'm hoping will be different this year. But it's got to help that we'll be working together, right? We'll have plenty of opportunities to be alone together. In enclosed spaces, just the two of us.

I catch a glimpse of him through the open window of the lifeguard station and smile. Like right now. Senior year business is the perfect excuse for us to be alone—

I stop short in the doorway.

I just barely hold back a groan as I realize that Ben *is* waiting for me.

But so is Ryan.

TWO

Ryan

THE WAY MARA'S face falls whenever she sees me is almost funny.

Almost.

I'd be offended if I wasn't so used to it. But I've come to expect her disdain, and so I greet her scowl with a big smile that I know is gonna drive her nuts. "There she is. Mara Loman, the woman of the hour."

Her eyes narrow and I swear I can see her brain working, trying to figure out if I'm mocking her and why.

But then she switches her attention to Ben, who's standing on the far side of the room, and her whole expression softens in that way it does around people she likes.

Which is basically everyone but me.

"Hey, Mara." Ben's all eager beaver over here. He looks way too excited to see Mara, even if she is looking extra pretty in a sundress.

When did she have time to shower and change? I

narrow my eyes even further, my gaze catching on her lips. Is she wearing lip gloss? My brows draw down as I watch her and Ben make small talk and laugh.

No. Mara's not laughing, she's...she's giggling. My jaw drops in shock and awe.

She *giggled*.

She doesn't blush and stammer, but there's something so very girly about the way she tucks her hair back behind her ear. There's something almost...flirty in the way she tilts her head to the side to listen as he talks.

What the...

What is *happening* here?

"I set up that group Facebook page for our class like we'd talked about," Ben's saying. I'd tuned him out for a while because they were giving new meaning to the word *boring* as they talked about student council crap.

"Great!" Mara's face lights up like this truly is great news. Like Ben just established world peace over here.

"What do we need a group page for?" I asked.

Two pairs of eyes swing my way. Both of them blink as if they're surprised to find me there. I straighten from where I'd been leaning against the office's desk. Yeah, that's right. I'm right here.

Mara's brows knit together, and that sweet little smile she'd been wearing fades fast. "Ryan, what are you doing in here?"

She glances up at the clock at the same time I inform her, "My shift's over."

Her gaze drops down to mine and...she's pissed. I can see it. I can feel it. Beneath that pretty, girl-next-door face and the big, blue eyes, lives a permanently pissed off, judgmental, competitive, grudge-holding beast. But apparently, I'm the only one who can see her.

Lucky me.

"That doesn't answer the question. What are you doing here?" she asks again, this time with a pointed glance toward Ben, who's looking something up on his phone.

"Just signing out for the day," I say.

I should leave. I should walk out. But it's way more fun to hang around and watch her blow a fuse while she tries to glare me out of the office.

Ben's done with whatever he was doing on his phone, so now his attention is back on Mara, which means she's once more a smiley sweetheart.

Ha! Please.

The girl is as sweet as a lemon, and with just as much sense of fun.

"Elijah's really into it," he's saying. I start to pay attention again because if this involves Elijah, then it most likely involves a party or some very poor decisions.

"A scavenger hunt?" Mara says, her brows drawn together in confusion and her voice filled with wariness.

I straighten. "He's actually going through with it?"

Mara and Ben look at me with that blank expression again. Seriously? I'm six feet tall with muscles to spare. I'm kinda hard to miss. But Mara blinks at me like she's hoping I'll dissolve into thin air if she ignores me long enough.

Nice try. I'm pretty sure she learned her lesson in junior high that ignoring me is not the answer. I don't like being ignored, almost as much as I dislike being glared at all the time by Miss Bossypants over here.

Elijah's on the football team with me. We're buddies. I have no idea why they're surprised I know about this.

"Yeah," Ben says, turning back to Mara. "He's really into it."

"So, like, in addition to the end of the year scavenger

hunt?" She looks so perplexed it's kind of cute. The girl can't even imagine why someone would break tradition and do something non-school related.

"She's not going to play," I say to Ben.

His lips turn down in annoyance and she shoots me a glare. "How do you know?"

"Because I've seen the list, Sunshine," I tell her. "It's not your beat."

Now I have two nerds staring at me in confusion. "It's not exactly school-sanctioned," I say. I watch her reaction closely. "Not everything on the list is on the up and up."

Her lips part, and I see it in her eyes. She gets what I'm saying, and she knows I'm right. We both know that hell will freeze over before Mara Loman breaks a rule, let alone a law.

Not that there's anything seriously dangerous or illegal on the list, but it's not for a goody-two-shoes like Mara, either.

"Yeah, I guess that's true," Ben says. He looks uncomfortable as he glances over at Mara. "But if you want to help me, I'd—"

"There's a cash prize though." I interrupt before Ben can finish, and I don't even know why. It's not like I don't like Ben. He seems decent enough, and I know he's buddies with Elijah so he can't be a total loser.

Besides, I'm not a rude guy. Not really.

Well, not usually.

But I really want Mara to do this scavenger hunt. I'd kill to see her come down off her high horse and break a rule or two.

Okay fine, I want to knock her off that high horse with a two-by-four and watch her come crashing to the ground.

And unlike Ben, I know exactly how to get her on board.

They're both staring at me again, but Mara's eyes have that gleam I know well. She's thinking. Calculating. "How much money?"

Honestly, I have no idea. I'd just heard him throw out the idea the other night when we were partying up at the lake and the numbers he was tossing out there made my jaw drop. We hear voices coming from down the hall and I recognize one. "Let's ask him, shall we?" I lean into the hall. "Yo, Eli!"

I freeze at the sight before me.

Oh crap. No, no, no. Not today. I'm about to duck back into the office but I'm not quick enough.

"Ryan! Hi!" Leah's waving frantically like I'm going off to sea and this is our final farewell.

I try not to cringe. "Hey, Leah."

"Leah's here?" Ben says. Next thing I know Ben and Mara are right behind me in the doorway so I can't escape.

Elijah's cousin is the sweetest person I have ever met. I'm almost positive it's all genuine, too. She's just...nice.

So. Freakin'. Nice.

This would normally not be an issue. I have nothing against nice people. But she's so obviously into me, and I just don't feel that way about her.

She's nice—wait, did I say that already? She's pretty. She's smart. And she's going back to wherever it is she lives during the year just as soon as the school season starts up.

So this means I only have a few more weeks of avoiding awkward one-on-one conversations with weirdly mean-ingful eye contact. I can deal with that.

Sure enough, the sight of Leah even has Mara smiling as Elijah and I talk about the pool's upcoming end of season party. I've worked here as a lifeguard for years—Mara too—and before that I'd been coming here as a member with my family, so I know the drill. During the day it's the big guest event of the year, but after the pool closes, it's notoriously the most epic staff party of the summer. Even the most hardass of managers look the other way.

Some even join in.

I glance over Mara. Even the great and saintly Mara might let down her guard and have some fun. *Gasp!* I know, right? The mere thought is alarming.

"I can't believe you're actually giving a few grand to the winner of this thing," I say loudly when Elijah hands over the list he'd printed out.

"A few *grand?*" Marah squeaks behind me.

Elijah shrugs. "Maybe."

Yeah, Elijah's rich like that. He makes my family seem down on their luck, and I've got a doctor for a mother and a lawyer for a dad, not to mention we live in one of those big houses on the hill.

"I haven't decided on the amount yet. Depends on how much money will ensure the players are properly motivated." Elijah says this in the slow, lazy drawl that is so very him. At first glance, with his heavy-lidded stoner vibe, one might think he's not paying attention, or maybe that he's just really apathetic. But that's not the case at all.

He's always got an agenda, and I have no doubt this scavenger hunt is part of it.

Mara's asking questions. Lots of questions. The mention of a cash prize has lit a fire in her, just like I knew it would

I smirk down at the list. Do I know how to play this girl or do I know how to play her? To be fair, if you know a person long enough, you know what makes them tick.

And I've known Mara forever.

Poor Ben's only known her since he transferred in a couple years ago. He couldn't possibly know that the only way to Mara's heart is to start talking about scholarships and grant money. Or maybe planners. I'd bet my summer's salary that the girl gets hot for planners.

"We're heading out to that pizza place down the street. You guys want to come?" Elijah asks.

Ben's already joining them, because apparently Ben and Elijah are better friends than I'd realized. Or maybe he's friends with Leah.

Probably. Leah's the kind of girl who's friends with everyone. She only comes to stay with Elijah's family for the summers, but I'm pretty sure she has more friends in this town than I do.

She turns her gaze to mine, and there is way too much eagerness there as she says, "Oh please come with us."

"I wish I could," I lie. "But my folks expect me home."

Her face falls. "Oh. Well, maybe I can stay and help you finish up—"

I cut her off with an exaggerated wince. "I wish you could but..." I nod in Mara's direction and give a grimace of regret again. "My boss here needs to see me."

Mara doesn't notice because she's too busy smiling and laughing at something Ben said.

"Right, Sunshine?" I drape an arm across her shoulders and Mara flinches.

"What?" Her smile fades to a sneer in a heartbeat, and she glances pointedly at my arm like it's a boa constrictor she wants dead.

"You still need to see me after work?" I ask. I grin down at her look of confusion. "I was just telling Leah how we have some business to finish up here so—"

"Oh, but—"

I cut off her protest by loudly saying our goodbyes. Elijah, Leah, and Ben head out before she can stop them.

Mara whips around and smacks my arm so hard I drop it. "What are you doing?"

"Saving you," I lie.

She blinks. "Saving me? From what?"

I shrug. "You like Ben, right?"

"*What?*" Her voice is louder and sharper, but I don't miss the telltale blush in her cheeks.

Mara Loman is blushing. Will wonders never cease.

"It's obvious that you do," I say.

She jerks back a bit, and I feel a kick of guilt at the uncertainty in her eyes. But she rebounds quickly. "So what if I do?"

I head back into the office and fall into the seat, making it roll backwards. "Can I give you some advice?"

"No."

I ignore that. "There's this thing called playing hard to get." I arch my brows. "Ever heard of it?"

She rolls her eyes. "I don't want to *play* anything."

"That's exactly your problem," I say.

"I don't have a problem."

"You don't have Ben, either," I say.

She makes a noise that's like an old man's harrumph and that makes me laugh. I can't help it. It's freakin' cute when she's an angry old man.

"Why are you laughing?'

I lean forward. "Do you remember those old dudes in The Muppets?"

She frowns. "Statler and Waldorf?"

I stare at her for a long moment. "Why do you know that?"

She waves off the question. "What's your point."

I shake my head. "I don't remember."

She crosses her arms. "Better question. Why did you cockblock me just now?"

I widen my eyes and slap a hand over my mouth in feigned horror at her language. She rolls her eyes.

Sometimes it feels like she and I have been playing out this little routine of ours for so long that we could do it in our sleep.

She tilts her head to the side, but it's not that cute, flirty move she'd done with Ben. She's eyeing me with suspicion. "What do you want, Ryan?"

I throw my hands out wide. "I'm just trying to help."

"I don't need your help," she says.

"Don't you?" I give her an admittedly condescending little smile and it makes her eyes light with fire. Just like I knew it would.

"I don't."

I kick my legs out in front of me, my fingers steepled together in front of my chest. "How many boys have you dated, Mara?"

"*Pshh.*" Her exhale of disgust is so hard it sends her wispy, blonde, half-dry hair out of her face.

"That's not an answer."

"I don't need your help," she says.

"Mara, honestly..." I arch my brows. "Have you ever even kissed a guy?"

Her eyes widen and her cheeks are so red it looks painful. I figure that's my answer.

"Of course I have."

I press my lips together and fix her with another condescending smirk guaranteed to make her fume. "Mara," I say like a parent talking to a fibbing toddler.

She huffs. "I have."

She's a terrible liar.

I glance over at the first-aid station behind us. "The CPR dummy doesn't count."

She narrows her eyes but ignores the taunt. "You did not send them away just to help me get the guy."

The guy. *The guy?* Since when has Ben freakin' Harrow been *the guy?* I narrow my eyes right back. "How well do you even know this Ben character?"

She shakes her head. "Why do you make it sound like he's some stranger. He's been in our class for two years."

"Exactly. Two years is nothing at Lakeview," I shoot back.

This is true. Most of us were born and raised here in this Upstate New York lake town and we know everything there is to know about each other and our families.

Hooray for small towns, am I right? There are no secrets.

"You are insane," she says. "Ben is a nice guy."

"Nice," I repeat in a mutter. "Nice is overrated."

"No, nice is underestimated—" she says.

"Says the girl who is not nice," I interject.

"I am too nice!" She shouts this at the top of her lungs in frustration.

The silence that follows is pretty fantastic.

"Yes," I say after a beat. "Your yelling has convinced me. What was I thinking? Of course you're nice."

"I'm nice to the people who deserve it," she snaps.

And there you have it, folks.

I smirk. This is the truth of how Mara feels about me. And I'm not sure I can say she's wrong. She decided I wasn't good enough ten years ago and nothing I say or do now will change that.

I should let it go. I should get up, walk out, head home and—

"You ready for the staff race next week?" I ask.

She stills. It's a taunt and she knows it. The end of season party is all about the races. There's kids' races, staff races, fun races where people have to wear a ton of layers or walk on their hands...

The tension in this office makes me want to laugh.

"I'm going to win," she says.

"You're going to *try*," I correct.

"You're going to cheat," she says.

I roll my eyes. "I was eight."

"You were not eight last summer."

Fair enough. I hold my hands up. "You say cheat, I say play to win. Let's agree to disagree."

She holds my stare for so long I can hear the second hand of the clock tick by in the silence. Finally, she breaks it with a loud exhale and I can see her attempting to be mature and rise above.

That makes me want to drag her back down. I feel the most wicked urge to taunt her again, to remind her of how she has yet to win against me. But instead, I say, "I'll tell you what. Win or lose in the race, I'll still help you with your guy troubles."

"I don't have guy troubles." Her nostrils flare and her eyes grow bright.

"Uh oh," Celia says as her gaze goes from Mara to me.

I give her a little wave. "Hey, Celia."

She flashes me an answering grin. See? I'm not evil. Celia likes me. Actually, most people like me. Not to brag, but...most *girls* like me, in particular.

Just not this one. I look back to a still-fuming Mara who might as well have smoke coming out her ears.

"Come on," Celia said, dragging Mara out the door by her elbow. "Let's get you out of here before someone gets murdered."

Mara starts to leave but turns back to jab a finger in my direction. "For your information, the only guy trouble I have is *you*."

THREE

Mara

"GET your head in the game, Loman." Celia grips me by my shoulders as the crowd of fellow staff members around us cheer on the next swimmers in this relay.

Celia's in my face and scowling, and I think maybe she's trying to look fierce but she's too cute to pull it off. She looks like an angry bunny instead.

I swipe a hand over my face to wipe away some of the water dripping into my eyes. "But he cheated," I say, my voice annoyingly high and tight with anger. "Again."

She rolls her eyes, and when I start to look over at the next lane over, she grips my cheeks and keeps my head centered so I can't look over.

I don't need to though. I can hear Ryan laughing.

Prick.

"Every year," I mutter. "Every freakin' year he does this to me."

"I know, I know." Celia sighs loudly. "But dude, this is

not the Olympics. I mean, just look at what is going on right now."

She spins me around to face the pool, and it's admittedly...not serious. The next group of lifeguards are paddling atop inflatable animals. Derek, the lifeguard on my team, is furiously kicking atop an oversized duck, and it's impossible not to laugh at the sight.

"See?" Celia says in triumph when I start to chuckle. "We all saw Ryan hold you back, but it's just a game. It's supposed to be fun."

I start to grudgingly agree, but the sound of his voice next to me stops me short.

"Nice try, Celia," Ryan says. "But nothing is just a game with this one, and we all know Mara doesn't know how to have fun."

I stiffen, and behind me Celia sighs. "Do you mind, Ryan? I'm trying to keep you from being murdered over here."

He laughs. "I don't know why you try."

"I don't either. I should leave you to your fate."

"You wouldn't." He pretends to be horrified, but I don't need to look over to know that he's grinning. Stupidly pleased with himself for winning and even more elated that he's beaten me.

"I would," Celia says. "You know you don't *have* to antagonize her, right? You could try and be the bigger man, just once." But her tone is all light and happy. Celia has no issue with Ryan. I don't get how she can find him so amusing, but I've stopped trying to understand ages ago.

"I could," he agrees. "But where's the fun in that?"

I tune them out, cheering on Derek instead, and bursting out in a laugh when his duck rolls over and he goes under.

Our team loses, which delights the heck out of Ryan, and we all head back to the locker rooms to dry off and clean up. I'd normally do a quick shower to rinse off the chlorine and then tie my hair up and be out of here, but Celia and a few of the other girls on the staff are not okay with this plan.

"You, me, my makeup bag. Now," my friend Bethany says, waving a little beige bag in my direction. She's one of the daughters of the club, as I like to think of them.

It's a whole different breed altogether, these kids who grew up coming here as guests and now work here part-time. They're not like me—someone who actually had to go through multiple rounds of interviews and fill out all the applications. People like Bethany and Ryan had a word spoken on their behalf by their parents, and *boom*. A summer job appears, complete with the best shifts and the most accommodating hours. The special treatment is subtle, but it's there. Though I'm not sure they even realize it.

But Ryan consistently showing up late, for example? I couldn't get away with that. Or, maybe I *could* but I wouldn't try because, unlike him, I could be fired.

But despite being a club member, Bethany's a sweet girl and she's heading back to university in a couple of days, so I enjoy this little alone time together as she does my makeup and tells me all her plans for the next year at school.

By the time she's done, I feel...well, mildly ridiculous, to be honest. I'm not a big makeup person, and while she assures me I don't look like a clown, I kind of feel like one.

"You look hot," she says as she shoves me through the door. "Now promise me you're going to have fun tonight."

Bethany's the one who nicknamed me *the pool mom* my first summer working here. She always laughs when she says it, and it's usually said with affection by the rest of the staff, so I'm not complaining. And besides, I can't help it if I worry about people. And it's not my fault that I'm the one people tend to seek when they need a shoulder to cry on or someone to help with their problems. But even so...

When she shoves me out the door, I'm on board with the plan to let my pool mom duties slide for one night. I've worked my butt off all summer, and this is the one night I'm not expected to be on point.

I hear the music coming from the pool area before I step outside, and I'll admit it—I'm a little excited for this party. Sure, there's a part of me that tenses up at the thought of all the trouble that could occur and the rules we're violating, but it's tradition. Like senior skip day, the lifeguards, staff, and their friends having a rager on the last week of summer vacation is expected. Encouraged, even.

And besides, it's kind of awesome to be here after hours like this. Someone has strung up Christmas lights around the pool, and a Spanish song with a totally danceable beat is blaring over the speakers.

There's a keg, which I avoid, and a table full of food that the club provided.

See? If there was ever any doubt that this was a club-sanctioned event, this just cinched it. They provide the catering, for heaven's sake.

My phone buzzes in the back pocket of my jeans, and I know who it's going to be before I pull it out. Sure enough, I see my mom's name next to a text telling me to have fun, be safe, and to not do anything she wouldn't do. This is followed by a winky-face emoji because we both know I'd never do half the stuff she's done in her lifetime.

She'd been a wild child, and I am the consequences.

"Oh, thank goodness you're here," Celia says in a rush when I reach her. She latches onto my arm the second I rejoin the party, and I know before she says it that Heath is here.

"It's going to be okay," I say slowly, trying my best to ignore the fact that her nails are digging into my skin. What's more important here is that Celia looks two seconds away from hyperventilating. "Where is he?" I ask. I'm using a low, calming tone because it's best not to startle Celia when she's in full crazyface mode.

How the girl survives going to the same school as Heath is a mystery. What's even more confusing is how she's been going to school with him for so long and still reacts this way.

Like a crazyface.

"He's over by the keg," she hisses, her eyes wide and locked on mine like we're having a staring contest I'm unaware of.

"All right," I say slowly. I know better than to look over toward the keg. I'll get yelled at. So instead, I try to present reasonable options. "We could either walk past the keg and say hello—"

"No! Are you kidding me?" She sounds so horrified I might as well have suggested we strip naked and streak the party. "He's with *her*."

I wince on Celia's behalf. Lakeview High's favorite brooding basketball star has been on-again off-again with mean girl supreme Pamela Casey for years now. If they're back together, that explains why Heath is here since Pamela works part-time at the driving range.

They have one of those completely confusing, seemingly toxic relationships that are impossible to keep up with. It's also the reason Celia has an ulcer. It's bad enough that her crush is ridiculously hot and looks so serious all the time, but it's also impossible to tell if and when he's single.

"Here's what we'll do," I say in my best soothing tone.

She nods furiously, clearly eager for my solution as her nails dig in deeper.

"We'll walk very slowly in the opposite direction," I say, taking absurdly slow steps toward a group gathered on the far side of the pool by some tables that had been set up for beer pong.

"Okay, good idea," she says.

If anyone finds it odd that Celia and I are holding one another and creeping toward the far end of the pool like a couple of cat burglars, they don't say anything. And by the time we reach the others—far away from Heath and Pamela—Celia's come back to her senses.

"Wow," she says with a giant sigh as she flashes me a relieved smile. "Thank you."

I wrap an arm around her shoulders and squeeze. "You're welcome."

I can't say I understand her weirdness around Heath. Honestly, I can't imagine freaking out over any guy just because I have the hots for him, but that's just one of many ways in which Celia and I are very different. We like to say that our differences are what make us such a great team, and it's times like this that I believe it. We always have each other's backs.

Even as I think it, Celia proves my point by stepping in front of me and holds her arms out like she's trying to take a bullet for me.

"Um, Celia? What are you doing?" I ask.

"Mara!" Ryan calls out my name.

I groan. Celia's not trying to physically protect me. My wonderful BFF is trying her best to shield me from view from my arch nemesis.

If only she wasn't shorter than me by a foot, her cunning

plan might have worked. As it is, she wrinkles her nose in regret as she glances up at me. "Sorry."

Ryan calls my name again, hailing me from where he's standing in the middle of a bunch of female staff members who are laughing over something he's said. No surprise there.

I shrug and sigh, giving Celia a resigned smile. "One day he'll be out of my life, right?"

"That's the spirit." She pats my shoulder in comfort as we head toward Ryan and his little harem. Seriously, I have no idea what all the girls at this club see in him. I mean, aside from the good looks. Obviously.

"You're just in time, Mara," he says.

"For what?" Celia asks.

"Beer pong competition!" Bethany calls this out, and I'm not sure how she managed to get drunk between doing my makeup three minutes ago and now, but it seems as though she's accomplished it.

Either that or she's just really embracing her inner sorority girl, because she then starts up a chant that has the rest of the party heading our way to see what the fuss is about.

"I don't drink," I say.

"Of course she doesn't," Ryan says with a smirk for the crowd. He turns back to me. "Likely excuse. If you're no good at the game, you can just say so—"

"I know what you're doing," I say. "And it's not going to work."

The trouble is—it always works. And he knows it. Even when I know he's goading me, I still feel that competitive pull. The urge to show him he's not the king of the universe and that I can do anything he can do.

And I can probably do it better.

Except for football, obviously. But I have zero interest in that sport.

Still, just because I feel the competitive draw doesn't mean I have to give in. Especially if it means doing something I don't feel comfortable doing—or even *want* to do. Blame it on my ultra-lax mother letting me take sips of her drinks whenever I was curious, but I just don't see the appeal of alcohol.

Blame it on holding Celia's hair back the last time she drank at a party, and I *really* don't understand the desire to partake in drinking games.

Ryan's eyes roam over my face, and for a second I wonder what he sees. I definitely wonder what he's thinking when his eyes darken and his gaze inexplicably drops to my mouth. "Okay, fine."

My eyes narrow because he's relenting way too easily. This is never a good sign. Last time he stopped goading me into a challenge, it ended with me being on the wrong end of a prank.

Granted, that had been in elementary school, but even so—life experience has taught me it's wise to be wary when Ryan concedes.

"I know you don't drink, so let's change it to straight up ping pong," he says.

A couple of people groan, but soon enough, they're all on board and a few of the girls rearrange the table and get out the paddles from the rec room.

"Two out of three," he announces, holding up one of the paddles like he's some announcer in a boxing ring.

Someone hands me a paddle, and I can't hide my grin. Not to brag, but I'm awesome when it comes to games like this. I have excellent hand-eye coordination, which is why

I'm the star pitcher for our softball team. "Get ready to lose," I say to Ryan as I go to take my spot.

But then he hands the paddle off to Bethany and I frown. "I thought I was playing you."

"You're playing *for* me," he says.

His cocky grin makes me freeze, and I frown over at him. "What does that mean?"

But then Celia blows a whistle—*my* whistle, which she must have snagged from the lifeguard station—and Bethany lobs the first ball.

I forget all about Ryan and his annoying smirk as I get into the game. It's been ages since I've played, and I'd forgotten how much fun it can be. I beat Bethany handily, and then it's one of the waitresses' turn. We're all laughing and trash talking, and most of the other girls are drinking as they play.

I'll admit, their drinking probably works to my advantage. The last one up is so tipsy she's barely even trying, and we spend more time falling over the table laughing than we do hitting the actual ball.

I'm having such a good time, I even manage to forget Ryan's there. And while I hear him laughing and chatting with the other girls, I'm content to ignore him and have some fun of my own.

"That's it!" Celia calls. She didn't play but has declared herself the official umpire. I didn't have the heart to tell her umpires in ping pong is not a thing.

Celia comes over and lifts my right hand over my head. "We have a winner!"

Everyone cheers and I launch into my happy dance— and yes, I do have a happy dance—and this makes us all laugh harder. Even Ryan's laughing when I glance up, and he's watching me like I'm the most entertaining thing he's ever seen.

Probably just storing up insults for later, but for a short time, there's peace in the kingdom and all is well.

"So?" I turn to face the others. "What do I win?"

I don't miss the looks that are exchanged, sneaky and wary and...

Oh no.

"What?" I ask, my happy dance coming to a faltering stop. "What's the prize?"

Ryan steps forward, throwing his arms out wide. "Congratulations, Mara. You won a kiss from yours truly."

FOUR

Ryan

ONCE AGAIN, I'd be offended by Mara's horror if it wasn't so freakin' funny.

"What?" Her voice is little more than a squeak. Celia winces in response.

I'm guessing Celia didn't realize what these girls were playing for either or she would have warned Mara.

"Kissing *you* is the prize?" Mara couldn't possibly look or sound more disgusted if she tried.

I shrug. "It wasn't my idea."

"It wasn't," Bethany says, thrusting herself into this conversation with a big grin. "It was my idea." She reaches up and presses my cheeks together so my lips automatically purse out like a fish. "Lizzie and I were talking about how we've always wondered what it would be like to kiss Mr. Hottie here."

My brows arch up. "Mr. Hottie, huh?"

At least that's why I attempt to say, but my face is still being manhandled so it comes out muffled.

"Please don't call him Mr. Hottie," Mara says with a weary tone that makes her sound seventy rather than seventeen. "It'll go to his head."

"Too late," I say as Bethany drops her hands.

"Well, forget it," Mara says, already backing away with her hands up, palms out like I'm some rabid dog that's about to lunge on top of her. "I'll forfeit the win."

"You?" My brows shoot sky high at that. "Wait a sec. Let me get this straight. *You*, Mara Loman, will actually give up the win just to avoid kissing me?"

Celia, Bethany, and a couple others are all watching her as she scowls. "I'm not giving up the win, I just don't want the prize."

"Uh huh." I rock back on my heels as I study her. "So what I'm hearing is, you're chicken."

"*What?*" Her whole face screws up and she plants her hands on her hips.

I wonder if she has any idea how cute she looks. Like a little kid having a temper tantrum. So...maybe cute isn't the right word. Funny, though. And exasperating. And maybe just a little adorable.

Or she would be if this temper tantrum wasn't because she's so disgusted by the thought of kissing me.

Yeah, it's possible my pride is stinging just a little over here.

She huffs. "Just because I don't want to kiss you doesn't mean I'm *afraid* of kissing you."

I move past Celia and Bethany and leave all the other girls behind as I step into Mara's space. She backpedals, and I follow until we're a few feet from the others giving us some semblance of privacy. "Look, I get it, Mara," I say. "I really do."

She narrows her eyes, but she can't argue when I'm agreeing with her. I see the flash of irritation in her eyes and just barely swallow a laugh. This girl is so crazy stubborn but also so very predictable.

Over the years, I've learned how to press her buttons, and these days, I'm something of a pro when it comes to irritating Mara.

I lean down slightly, and she pulls her head back like I'm going to kiss her right then and there even though she'd said no.

Please. I'm not that much of an ass.

"I think I know what the problem is," I say.

"That you're a conceited prick with an ego the size of Mount Everest?" she offers.

"You're afraid you're going to like it."

"You think I'm going to *like* kissing you?" She wrinkles her nose again. "Ew."

"*Ew?* Really?" I arch my brows. "Are you twelve years old?"

Her eyes narrow. "I know what you're doing."

A smile tugs at my mouth. Does she? I hope so, because I'm not so sure I know what I'm doing anymore. I mean, I know I'm goading her. I'm just...not entirely sure why.

My gaze falls to her lips. All I know is, this is yet another battle between us, and I want to win.

"You're trying to manipulate me," she says. "Make me feel like I have to kiss you to prove a point or something. But it's not going to work."

"What if I tell you *I* want to kiss *you*?" I say.

There's a gasp and some whispers from the group

behind me. I'm not sure how much our co-workers hear, but they sure as heck heard that.

I watch Mara's lips part in surprise. That shine from her lip gloss or whatever it is she's wearing makes her lips look even fuller and pinker and lusher than usual.

I feel a surge of something hot and tight in my lungs, and...oh crap.

I mean it. I want to kiss her.

I'd said it to tease her. I'd intended to throw her off guard. That comment was supposed to be just another tactic to get my way, except...*crap*.

I really do want to kiss her.

This realization is not exactly welcome. For either of us, if that flicker of disgust in her eyes is anything to go by.

She backs up another step. "You don't mean that."

I don't argue. I'm not sure I want her to know that I mean it. I shrug. "Don't tell me you've never thought about it."

She opens her mouth and shuts it. And when her gaze drops to my mouth, I feel it like a touch. My insides tighten and twist, my heart starts a painful thudding in my chest, because...

Aw hell. I'd been teasing, but she *has* thought about it. It's obvious in the way she didn't protest. She truly is a terrible liar, which is probably why she rarely lies. When she lies, I know it. And she *knows* that I know.

But also, I see it in her eyes—the way they darken, the flicker of curiosity, the flare of heat. It's there and gone in a heartbeat, and she's back to looking disgusted before I can blink.

But I saw it.

"I think I know the real issue here," I say. "You're scared because you've never been kissed before, right?"

Her eyes flare wide as she meets my gaze. "What? No." But the *no* is a little too quick. "I told you, I've—"

"And I don't believe you," I say.

Her cheeks turn pink. And holy crap if that doesn't make something in my chest tighten. I'm embarrassing her, and I don't mean to.

But I also know it's gonna get me what I want.

And I am just as much of a jackass as she thinks I am because I'm gonna do whatever it takes to win...like always.

"Look, I get it, Mara." I clap a hand to my chest like I feel her pain. "I wouldn't want to have my first kiss in public either. You're probably worried that you don't know how or you're really bad at it, and..." I shrug. "Maybe you are."

"I'm not." Her cheeks are bright red, and she's talking through clenched teeth.

She's just too freakin' easy to rile. If you're me, at least. I've honestly never seen her lose her temper with anyone else.

So, I guess that makes me special? Or just that much of a jerk that the kind, beloved mother-figure for all of Lakeview High loses her cool whenever I look in her direction.

"I know what you're doing," she says.

I grin. "Do you?"

"Just kiss him already," Bethany says.

I didn't even realize we still had an audience, and I'm guessing Mara didn't either judging by her shocked expression.

"It's not a big deal," someone else calls out. "It's just a kiss."

My gaze never leaves Mara's face, so I see it. The slight wince with those words. Just a kiss.

It's just a kiss unless she makes a big deal out of it.

It's just a kiss unless it's her *first* kiss.

It's just a kiss...with the one guy she can't stand.

I should let her off the hook. I should be a bigger person and forget about the fact that I'm dying to kiss this girl—just to satiate my curiosity, that's all. I should turn around and make a joke and let her walk away from this moment with her pride intact.

But I don't move. Not right away. I'm stuck there watching this play of emotions in her eyes, and it's mesmerizing.

The flare of guilt starts to outweigh my curiosity as I watch her sort through her own inner battle.

That's it. I don't know why I want to kiss her so badly, but I can't force her hand. I start to turn away to let her off the hook, but at the same time, she lets out an exasperated sigh. "Oh, what the hell."

That and a rousing round of applause are the only warning I get before Mara takes two steps toward me, plants her hands on my chest, bounces up on her tiptoes and kisses me.

Heat jolts through me at the first feel of her warm, soft lips against mine.

This isn't a kiss.

Kiss definitely isn't the right word for it.

I've kissed girls before, and this electric sensation that zaps through me from my lips to my head to me toes?

This is like nothing I've ever felt before. It's pure heat, and the feel of her lips on mine makes me instantly hungry, insatiable for more. It's overwhelming and intense, especially given the fact that she hasn't moved her lips at all.

She's pressing her lips against mine like she's getting this over with as quickly as possible and is determined not to enjoy it.

I don't think so.

I wrap my arms around her waist and tug, closing the distance she's trying to keep between us. Because...*hell*. If this is my one chance to kiss Mara Loman, I'm going to do it right.

Not that I've been obsessing over this or anything. I haven't.

But I have thought about it. And the reality is like nothing I ever could have anticipated.

Her body is lean and long and perfect. She fits against me like we were built to be one. And when I slide my lips over hers, shifting from what began as an aggressive peck to an *actual* kiss...

It's heaven.

Her lips part, and mine fit against them, molding to hers. When her lips part further on a gasp for air, I slide my mouth over hers, caressing and tasting. Savoring the heat and the taste and the scent of her that's wrapped around me like a cocoon.

But then she's kissing me back, tentatively at first and then a little deeper until I'm dizzy with wanting. Heat builds between us to the point that I can't think, I can't breathe...and I sure as hell can't remember why this is a bad idea.

When her hands move, sliding over my chest and up to my shoulders, I groan. The sound has her pulling back with a start.

Her gaze meets mine, and she looks as shocked as I feel.

I'd wanted to kiss her, I can admit that. If I'm being totally honest, I've been curious for a while now about what she'd feel like in my arms.

I've wondered even longer than that about how it would feel if she looked up at me like *this*—all heavy-lidded and sexy.

All vulnerable and sweet.

And for one heartbeat, there's no anger or judgment there in her eyes.

My chest feels like someone just took a chisel to it and split it in two. There's a crack in my ribs, and all I want to do is lean down and kiss her again.

But she's backing away, and all at once, I remember that we have an audience.

An audience that's laughing and teasing and...

Oh crap.

I run a hand through my hair as Mara turns and walks away. Her spine is straight, her shoulders squared. Celia's at her side.

I watch until they round the corner to another section of the club. I watch to see if she'll turn back, but she doesn't.

I stand there for a while, not really paying attention to anything going on around me, and long after the girls who'd been playing ping pong lose all interest in games.

"Dude, what are you doing over here?" My friend Heath is at my side, and I didn't even see him approach.

"Hmm? Oh, nothing, just..." I hold up my cup. "Just having a drink."

He looks from me to the empty space where I've been staring for way too long. "I think you've had enough, bro. You look like you're in a trance."

I give my head a shake, take a deep breath, and force a laugh. "Just bored, I guess." I look around with open skepticism. "I thought this was supposed to be a party."

"Yeah, well, I hear there's an afterparty at Bethany's house."

I nod.

"Do I want to know why everyone's talking about you and Mara?" Heath asks.

I glance over at my friend, who's not nosy and definitely not prone to questions. But I know he likes Mara. Not in a *like*-like way, just in a he-respects-her way. And vice versa. They're both serious people, just in different ways. He's the broody silent type to her more neurotic type-A vibe. But they both take everything too seriously.

Like that kiss.

I take a swig of my drink. My guess is she's overanalyzing the crap out of that kiss.

Not like me. I turn to my friend with a grin. No use thinking about a kiss—no matter how hot—if it's never going to happen again, right?

"You going to the afterparty?" he asks. "I hear Leah's going to show with Elijah."

I wince and my buddy laughs softly under his breath. "Why don't you just go out with the girl and get it over with? It's not like she's looking for longterm. She's leaving in a couple weeks, isn't she?"

I shrug. Somehow it feels wrong to go out with her knowing she likes me and I don't feel the same. Even if it is short-term, it would be a lie I can't keep up, and the idea of hurting a sweet girl like that is unthinkable.

I have this flicker of guilt because...had I just hurt Mara?

I don't think so.

I hope not.

"Okay, seriously, you're freaking me out," Heath says as he watches me. "I'm the one who broods around here, not you."

My head falls back with a genuine laugh. "You're right. I'm shaking it off."

"Shaking what off?"

I ignore the question. "So, you and Pamela, huh?"

He shrugs, and I just barely hold back a sigh. It sucks watching my friend get hurt over and over again, but he's not a kid and I've got girl problems of my own.

I don't even realize I'm staring at the place where Mara had disappeared again until Heath claps a hand on my shoulder. "I don't know what happened between you two, man, but she's long gone."

Who? I should ask that, but neither of us would believe I don't know who he's talking about.

Mara's gone. She's long gone.

And who can blame her?

FIVE

Mara

TWO DAYS later I'm on my faded and worn living room couch trying my best to ignore Celia as she fills in our friend Addie about the kiss that shall not be named.

Okay, fine. The kiss with Ryan. Obviously. There are no other kisses to talk about because there are no other kisses. Period.

That kiss with Ryan was my first kiss. So yes, I am a liar. A big, fat liar. And the worst part? I don't even know why I felt compelled to lie.

I bury my head deeper in the book that I'm supposed to have done for summer reading before school starts next week. I'm in AP English, and the teacher is no joke. But who can focus on depressing, turn-of-the-century Russian literature when one's best friend is giving another friend a play-by-play of my first kiss.

With Ryan.

I close my eyes with a soft groan. My first kiss wasn't

supposed to be with Ryan, it was supposed to be with Ben. The guy I like. The guy I've spent a year getting to know, the guy who I have so much in common with, the guy who's nice to me and who makes me smile and laugh.

Not the jerk I can't stand.

I still can't believe I let him goad me into it. I don't know what I'd been thinking. And the worst part...?

"It was *hot*," Celia gushes, in what I presume is supposed to be a whisper but I can hear every word they say.

"Really?" Addie's curled up on the other side of the couch, her knees tucked up under her flowy floral skirt. She sighs as she leans forward so her elbows are on her knees and her chin rests on the palm of her hand, the very picture of a captive audience member. "I always miss all the fun."

Addie's been going off to stay with her dad every summer since we were kids. She spends most holidays there too, so we never get to hang out with her when school's out.

This last week of summer vacation is all we have left, but I mean to make the most of it. I'm only working part-time now that the pool's hours have changed. They'll be closing the outdoor pool for good after Labor Day. But for now, I have a lightened work schedule, and a little free time before I dive into the school year.

I give up on trying to read any more. Seriously, who can read when one's first kiss is being replayed and overanalyzed? And instead, I pull out a slip of paper I'd printed out.

It's the list of scavenger hunt items, and I can admit...reading it gives me hives.

I mean, get an application from a strip club? Okay. I can handle that. Granted, the thought of going into the one and only strip club in town makes me squirm, but I can do it. But twerking on a statue? What does that even mean? And getting someone's butt cheek signed by a stranger? That's just gross. Right?

"I always knew it," Addie's currently whispering back to Celia.

And I use the word *whispering* in the broadest of ways.

"Always knew what?" I ask.

Addie shoots me a sidelong look, tucking her long auburn hair back behind her ear. "That you and Ryan have chemistry."

I automatically scoff. "If by chemistry you mean explosions, then yes. Gasoline and fire."

Celia narrows her eyes. She's been nagging me ever since it happened to admit that the kiss had been hot.

Had it been hot?

Maybe. Okay, yes. But mainly it had been terrifying. And confusing.

Also, unwanted. I mean, I didn't *ask* to feel sparks when we kissed. Shouldn't I have a say in who makes this body spark like that?

And yes, fine. There had been sparks. Firecrackers plus dynamite plus downed wires kind of sparks. The kind of sparks that fry your brain and burn you to the core.

The dangerous kinds of sparks.

I sit up a little straighter and take a deep breath. "It doesn't matter if there was chemistry or not because it can never happen again."

I'm met with two wide-eyed stares. Perhaps I'd said that a little too loudly and with way more intensity than necessary. I give a small conciliatory smile. "Too much?"

"I think we get the gist," Celia says.

Addie reaches for the book she's brought for what is ostensibly a study session, but which has turned into a gossip fest as Celia caught Addie up on all the happenings from this summer.

We'd talked to Addie often with videocalls and texts, but it's not the same as actually having her here. But Addie might be even more studious than I am, so she's the one who suggested our first hangout together be to get ahead of schoolwork.

Celia's the only one who didn't even pretend she's here to study. She showed up without a single book or laptop to her name. Even now, as Addie and I dive into our respective assignments, she's scrolling through social media on her phone. When she gasps aloud, I lift my head, and Addie does the same.

"Um..." Celia winces as her gaze meets mine. "Don't freak out, okay?"

I set my book down gently, my stomach twisting into a knot.

Addie speaks up. "You know, telling someone not to freak out is pretty much the best way to ensure they *do* freak out."

I nod as my pulse ratchets up a notch. "What is it?"

I think I already know. Or at least I suspect. Because there is literally only one human on the planet who can make me freak out. It's his superpower. He is the only person who can make my rational, well-balanced, and mostly-kind brain rage out like the Hulk with a mere smirk.

"What did he do?" I'm pleasantly surprised by the calmness in my voice...until Celia hands over her phone and I see the picture.

A let out a shriek that has my cat leaping across the room in terror before clapping a hand to my mouth.

Addie takes the phone from me. "Oh," she breathes. "Oh my." She turns to Celia. "That *does* look hot."

I snatch the phone back because as much as I don't want to see, I can't look away. Especially from the comments below.

His comments.

"I am going to kill him," I mutter through my hand, which is still over my mouth as if I can hold in this horror.

The picture is bad. Like, explicit and awful. It makes it look like whoever took this photo came upon the two of us when we were hot and heavy and...really kissing.

I mean, yes. We had really kissed. But it wasn't real. And he knows that. Yet that didn't stop him from joining in on the comments beneath. Most were fire emojis, some were semi-raunchy jokes, but most were questions. Like, for example, are they a couple now?

And the answer, obviously, is no.

But is that what Ryan says? Oh no. Nope. That moron has to go and crack jokes, calling me his girl and claiming we've been in love all this time.

He's kidding. *I* know he's kidding—in his terrible sense of humor kind of way. But does everyone else?

Does *Ben?*

"At least he wasn't the one who posted the picture," Addie says.

Like Celia, Addie has nothing against Ryan. They don't understand our hate-hate relationship any more than I do. I wish I could explain to them exactly why he gets under my skin, but it's just one of those things. Maybe it's chemistry. Or pheromones.

Or maybe I just see past his good looks to the evil soul beneath.

Either way, normally it irks me when Addie and Celia come to his defense, but right now...she has a point. For the first time, I take in more than just the photo and Ryan's comments. I see that it's this girl Bianca who posted it. She's a Lakeview High student, and this summer was her first time working at the club.

Apparently she hadn't yet learned that what happens at the country club stays at the country club. In her defense, she posted it with a bunch of heart emojis and a comment about how cute it was to finally see us get together.

Ugh. We are so *not* together. How did she think that just one kiss could undo a lifetime of animosity between us?

Clearly she's a romantic.

But those thoughts take a backseat once I realize where this is posted. It's not on Bianca's page. It's posted in the senior group that Ben created as part of our student council duties.

This is Ben's group.

Ben will see this. Ben may have *already* seen this.

I drop my head into my hands with a moan. Celia and Addie come over to my couch to comfort me. "This is supposed to be my chance," I whimper in self-pity. "Ben is supposed to notice me this year."

We'd spent a solid year getting to know one another, becoming friendly, ensuring we had things in common. And now this year was supposed to be the payoff. I was finally going to have a life outside of work and school. I was going to have the whole high school experience, complete with a boyfriend for the dances and all that stuff.

I have a plan, dang it. And this picture? It could destroy it.

"Ben's still going to notice you," Celia says with so much certainty I want to believe her.

"You think?" I ask.

Addie's nodding furiously. "Of course he will. Celia

says he came to the office at the pool and was flirting with you."

I nod as well, but I'm far less certain. I try to replay it all, recounting the scene to Addie in the process, and all I know is that he was friendly. He'd seemed happy to see me, and he'd invited me to work together with him on the scavenger hunt.

"That's something, right?"

"Totally!" She seems so certain, and Celia chimes in with more words of encouragement about how this picture fiasco is just a misunderstanding and it doesn't change anything.

I drop my head back against the couch with a sigh as I return to sanity. "Even if Ben doesn't return my feelings, it's fine, right? It's not like I need a guy."

"Of course you don't," Celia says.

"I've done just fine being single up until now," I add. And I have. I've barely given guys a thought until Ben came along, mostly because I've always had my priorities and having a boyfriend is not high up there on the list.

But you only do high school once, right? And I want to do it all. I don't want to miss anything. Not even the silly stuff like boys...and kisses.

Maybe that's why I caved when Ryan was pushing me to kiss him.

There was a little part of me that kept thinking, what if this is it? What if this is my one chance to be kissed before I go off to college?

Stupid, right?

But it's kinda the way it feels sometimes. Like time is running out. Like I'm going to blink and be done with school, out of this town, and onto a new life.

And I don't want to have regrets. I don't want to feel

like I've wasted time or missed out on the whole high school experience like my mom did when she got pregnant with me.

She's never once made me feel like she has regrets or that she resents me for ruining her fun—and truth be told, she didn't stop having fun. My early childhood is filled with memories of parties and laughter and adventures. But that's back when my dad was still around, and before money got so tight that she started working multiple jobs and I put all my focus into helping pay the bills and working my butt off for a scholarship.

My mom pokes her head into the living room now, flashing my friends a big grin. "Everything all right in here? I thought I heard a scream."

"Fine," I say automatically. I never want to add to my mom's worries. She's got enough on her plate.

But my mom looks to Celia and arches her brows. These two have a friendship all their own, and it almost always entails Celia ratting me out.

"Boy troubles," my bestie tells my mom.

Addie laughs beside me as I sigh and say, "Mom, don't get your hopes up—"

"You have a boyfriend?" she squeals.

Too late. Her hopes are officially up.

I shoot a glare at an unapologetic Celia. "No. I don't."

"But you like a boy," she says. The excitement in her expression is just too much to handle. There's expectations there, and I find myself shrugging in response.

"And?" she prompts.

And... I wish I have more to tell her. I wish I could make her day by saying I have the kind of high school life she's always wanted for me.

"And I'm working on it," I say, softening the words with

a smile that has her rolling her eyes as she heads toward the front door.

"Well, just promise me you'll have fun," she says. "And use protection!" she calls as she walks out.

"Thank you for that," I say in a dry tone to Celia.

She shrugs. "She worries about you. It's my job to make sure she knows that you're not working yourself into an early grave."

I laugh because she totally mimicked my mom's voice when she said that, and she does a great imitation.

To be clear, my mom appreciates how much I work, at my part-time jobs and at school. But it makes her sad too. If she tells me one more time how she wants me to have the whole teenager experience, I might scream.

It's not like I *don't* want that. I want it too. I've heard enough about my mom's regrets to know that I don't want to look back and feel like I missed out.

But I also want to keep my scholarship to Lakeview High, earn money for college, and keep up the grades to get into a good school.

I want it all, I guess. Is that asking for too much?

Maybe.

But whether it was my ideal kiss or not, at least I've been kissed now, right? That's something off the bucket list. And that's just the start. This year is going to be about more than just grades and college applications. This year I'm going to have it all if it kills me.

Which is why I decide right here and now that I'm going to do this silly scavenger hunt. Do I want the money? Yes. But I want the experience of it even more.

Somehow this decision helps me to settle down. Maybe this still won't be the year I get to see what the whole dating thing is all about, but at least I'll be doing something new.

Not that I'm giving up on Ben. I'm not. Of course I'm not. I've had a crush on him ever since we started chatting in biology last year. He has the perfect makings of a perfect first boyfriend.

I hand Celia's phone back to her.

I'll make sure Ben knows the truth. I'll make sure Ryan *tells* him the truth.

With a new plan in place, I start badgering Addie with questions about what Celia and I like to call her double life in Montana. She laughs and caves, telling us all about the new stepmother and the summer job she'd worked at an amusement park nearby.

Celia and I laugh and ask questions, but when Addie gets up to go to the bathroom, Celia leans in toward me with narrowed eyes. "You sure you're okay, Mara?"

I nod. "I'll be fine just as soon as I make this right."

"How are you going to do that?" she asks.

"Oh, *I'm* not going to do anything." I glance at her phone with a look of determination. "This is Ryan's fault, and he's going to fix it."

SIX

Ryan

LAKEVIEW HIGH IS SURPRISINGLY busy considering school isn't even officially in session yet. I've been stuck on the football field all afternoon, but I've seen handfuls of students going in and out of the school building, plus the other teams that started practices early. There's lacrosse players, soccer players, cheerleaders...

We're all burning alive in the late August sun.

I'm bent down, hands on knees, trying to catch my breath after Coach Lambert's grueling torture that he calls practice. I'd tried to stay in shape during the off season, but not even running every day before lifeguard duty or lifting weights after work made a bit of difference today.

I'm what you'd call wrecked.

"Man up, Hunter," Coach says as he walks past me with his roster, slapping my back hard on the way. "We need you in fighting form by next week."

I nod and grunt. It's the best I can do.

I'm also what you'd call the star of the team. And no, that's not my ego talking. That's just the fact of the matter. I'm not the quarterback but I'm on the starting lineup and, more importantly, I'm third generation. Not to mention, my three older brothers were all stars of the Lakeview team and led them to state finals every year they played.

Maybe this is why Coach is especially tough on me during practice. He, like my parents, seems to think I'm a carbon copy of my superhuman brothers who've gone before me.

And I try to be. Lord knows I freakin' try.

I'll bet all three of them would have made it through this first practice without breaking a sweat.

"Ry, check it out, man," our wide receiver Toby says. "Your girl's here to see you."

My girl? I tense because there's no doubt in my mind he's talking about Leah. I saw her here earlier, hanging out with some of the cheerleaders and watching our team from the sidelines. She's not just Elijah's cousin, she's his friend, so it makes sense that she's tagged along, I guess. I just wish she didn't watch *me* quite so closely.

And now, apparently, she wants to chat too. Awesome.

I try to rally. I really do. I'm not a jerk, and she's a sweet kid. I can be pleasant and make small talk for a little while. But I'm already making up excuses in my head of why I can't hang out after practice as I turn to face her.

Only...

Toby's not talking about Leah.

My breath whooshes out of me when I see Mara stalking toward me. The sight of her is a surprise, that's all. That's the only reason my heart picks up its pace again like I just got done with another round of sprints.

Her hair is pulled back in a ponytail, but the wind is

trying its best to mess up her neat hairdo, and a few locks escape, whipping in front of her face as she heads my way. She's smiling—but not at me. Oh no. Of course not. One of the cheerleaders said something to her so she's laughing as she calls something back. Then she's smiling at Elijah who walks up to her like it's his right.

A surge of possessiveness is so unexpected—and so unwelcome—it takes me a full second to remember that I have absolutely nothing to be jealous of. A, she means nothing to me. Obviously. But also B, Elijah would never go for a girl so straightlaced as Mara. And C, Mara would never be into a guy who lives to party and create chaos like Elijah.

Besides, I already know who Mara likes.

"Whoa, man. You all right?" Toby asks. He's a good kid. A junior. But I'm ready to punch him in the face when he says, "Did you and your girl split up already?"

Me and my girl. Ha. That's a laugh. Mara's not mine, and it's like she's making a point of proving that as she stands there laughing it up with Elijah, pushing her hair back from her face in a way that's...*sexy*.

Ah hell.

Not sexy. She's just being Mara. A laughing, smiling, *happy* Mara.

And that kiss has definitely messed with my head.

I go to tell Toby that he got it all wrong. We're not really together, I'd just let people think that to mess with Mara. But before I get the chance, Mara's turning away from Elijah, and heading my way.

I forget all about words as I watch her smile fade and that light in her eyes dim to a dark glare.

"Oh man," Toby drawls. "Whatever you did, you'd

better apologize. No one wants his girlfriend looking that mad."

She's not my girlfriend. That's what I should say. My comments on that photo were a joke, how do people not understand this? *It's all a mistake.* That's what I should say. But what *do* I say? "Hey, babe. You here to watch your man practice?"

I might as well have tased her. Mara's eyes go wide, and I choke on a laugh as she falters in her step, her cheeks bright red. But not because she's embarrassed that people are staring at her—at us. Oh no.

She's just pissed.

"Do not call me *babe*," she says as she draws near. "And we both know you're not *my man.*"

I grin in the face of her sneer. It's a smile guaranteed to make her anger ratchet up another notch or two...or ten.

She presses her lips together in what I can only describe as a snarl. I've seen her mad before—like, during every one of our interactions over the last ten years. But I've never seen her so angry that she can't form words. I'm not sure if I should be proud I've managed to rile her so badly or cover my junk in case I've pushed her to violence.

"Aw, I've missed you too, Sunshine," I say.

"What were you *thinking?*" she hisses.

I smirk because honestly? I don't know. It had started as a joke. I knew she'd flip when she saw that picture—which I didn't post, by the way—and I couldn't resist the urge to add to her horror.

In my defense, I didn't actually think anyone would believe it. I'd thought the sarcasm was obvious. *Of course* she's not my girlfriend. There's no way in hell we could be a real couple. We can't stand each other, everyone knows that.

But apparently they don't, because no one seemed to get that I was kidding.

"Why did you say we were a thing?" she demands.

I shrug and then I lie. Unlike Miss Goody Two Shoes here, I can lie. I'm actually pretty dang good at it. "I thought I was doing you a favor."

Her brows arch in clear disbelief. "Really? That's the excuse you're going with?"

I can feel the stares of my teammates and the cheerleaders. I move in closer and give my best sexy smile.

It makes her glare intensify by a million but no one else can see her expression, and I'd rather not let the entire world know that I'm currently having my ass handed to me by the school's revered Little Miss Perfect.

"I'm not sure why you're so upset." I throw my hands out wide and puff out my chest. "I basically just made you the most popular girl at Lakeview. Now every guy in this school is going to want you and every girl is going to want to be you."

Her brows come down and she looks at me like I'm speaking Greek. "Do you even hear yourself talk? You sound like a caricature of yourself."

I laugh. It's a genuine laugh because she's not wrong. And I'm one hundred percent playing up the a-hole jock persona to make her mad.

Why? Because making her mad is a hell of a lot more fun than apologizing for a joke gone wrong. And besides, I'm not totally wrong. "Look," I lean in closer and lower my voice. "You want Ben to notice you, right?"

Her nostrils flare as she draws in a deep breath. "That's exactly my point. Your stupid joke in the comments is ruining everything."

Well. At least *she* realized I'd been joking. But the fact that she's worried about what Ben thinks pisses me off.

I don't have anything against the guy. He seems decent enough and Elijah likes hanging out with him which means he can't be a total loser. But he's just so boring. Nice, maybe, but he has all the personality of plain yogurt, from what I can tell.

Mara would be miserable with a guy like that. Didn't she see that? There'd be no challenge, no excitement, no passion...

My mind flashes back to that kiss before I can stop it. This is a mistake, because now I can't stop my eyes from dropping down to her lips. I can't stop my body from having a visceral memory of the way it felt when she was pressed against me. And in my mind's eye, all I can see is that sweet, open look in her eyes when it ended.

I run a hand over my chest, like that's going to ease this tightness. Like it's today's workout that has my ribcage contracting and my heart going wild.

Yeah. Let's go with that.

"Why are you doing this to me?" She visibly swallows, her gaze sliding away from mine in a way that wrenches my gut. "I know we don't always get along. Or...ever. But I've never done anything to hurt you."

There's silence for a beat, and it just about kills me. An angry Mara I can handle, a feisty Mara I freakin' love. But this...? A sad Mara? A hurt Mara?

I've never done anything to hurt you.

Those words choke me. I'm freakin' suffocating on a wide open field.

"What about the time you punched me so hard I lost a tooth?" I ask.

She rolls her eyes, and my insides unclench a bit as the

close call with real emotions seems to pass. "I didn't *punch* you, I accidentally hit you. And it was a baby tooth that was already loose."

She says all this on autopilot because it's one of my favorite accusations to throw her way. One of the only times *she* was the one in the wrong and not me. And yes, it had been an accident, but when one is dealing with a goody two shoes, one must work with what one's got.

"Fine." I wave a hand in a magnanimous gesture. "I officially forgive you for knocking a tooth out."

Her gaze is nonplussed. "Thank you."

"And I will tell Ben that we're not actually a thing," I add.

Her brows hitch up in surprise and her eyes brighten. "Really?"

My heart gives a weird hitch at that look in her eyes. "Yeah, why not?" I look away. "It's not like I want people thinking we're together either." One side of my mouth curves up. "I *do* have a reputation to protect, you know."

That light in her eyes dims again and her lips thin into a scowl. "Fine. So we're agreed, then."

"We're agreed."

"Today," she says.

I frown. "Today? I don't even have his number—"

"He's here," she says.

"He's...here?" I turn to look around, eyeing the cheerleaders on the sidelines and my teammates who are lingering to talk to them. "Where?"

"He's setting up the yearbook office," she says.

I stare at her for a long moment. Part of me wants to make a joke at how lame this guy is that he shows up during his summer vacation to prep for his yearbook committee. But another part of me is hung up on how she knows this.

Does she talk to this guy? Are they, like...friends?

The thought kills any urge to joke around.

I arch my brows. "Are you stalking this guy, Loman?"

"Just tell Ben the truth," she says. "Tell him and everyone else that you were joking before people get the wrong idea."

"Too late," I say with a smug smile.

She gives me an exasperated sigh and starts to walk away. "Just do it."

"Fine." I can't stop myself. "Your loss though, babe."

Her shoulders tense, but she keeps going.

"You really got to work on playing hard to get," I continue.

She pretends not to hear me. Which is fine. It's great. This joke has run its course anyway.

Practice is over and I have places to be, so I head toward the school to get this over with. I don't have to. I shouldn't need to. But I can't quite shake that look in her eyes, like I'd honestly hurt her.

I know I'm no saint, but I'm not nearly as cruel as she seems to think, either. I'm almost at the side doors leading into the school when I hear my name.

I freeze, my stomach sinking.

Oh no. Not now. Seriously, this day could not get any worse.

"Hey, Ryan!" Leah shouts. "Wait up!"

I'd already paused at the sound of my name. To ignore her now and pretend I didn't hear would be too mean. I take a deep breath and force a smile before I turn to face her.

She bounds toward me, her dark hair swaying and her smile so big I'm pretty sure I can see her molars. Such a sweet kid. She's only one year younger, but she's a kid in my eyes. Innocent and sheltered and ridiculously sweet.

"Hi!" She's bouncing on her toes when she reaches me. "How was practice?"

Yeah, that's how energetic she is. She makes me feel ancient. I'm exhausted from Coach's workout and the hot sun isn't helping. I give the bare minimum of answers as she bombards me with small talk.

"I was actually looking for Ben," I say, already turning, ready to make my escape.

"Oh. Yeah, of course." She reaches out a hand and touches my arm. "I just wanted to say that I totally get it now."

I should walk away. But her smile is soft and her eyes are filled with affection and...

And I have no idea what we're talking about.

"You do?" I say for lack of anything better.

She nods. "I do, and I just want you to know that..." She draws in a big breath and lets it out in a rush. "I'm so happy for you. I really am."

"You are?" Yup. I am a master of dialogue over here. But honestly, what the hell is she talking about? And why is she giving me a sappy look like we're talking about something romantic or...

Oh.

Oh no.

She reaches for my hands and clasps them in hers. I am definitely not comfortable right now. I feel my face muscles cramping in what I imagine is a terrible attempt at a smile.

It might be a grimace.

She squeezes my hands and gives me a beatific smile. "You and Mara are perfect for each other. I can see that now."

I open my mouth and what comes out is a croak. "Uh..."

Her smile widens like I said something funny. "It's actually kind of a relief."

"It is?"

She nods. I wish like hell she'd stop gripping my hands. It's messing with my head and weirdly reminds me of saying grace at Grandma's before dinner.

"You know..." She dips her head, all shy and coy. "I've had such a crush on you for ages. Ever since I've started to come to Lakeview over the summers."

"Oh." That's all I've got. My brain is frozen in horror. This is my worst nightmare. I don't do talks. I'm not an emotions kind of guy.

Somebody please save me.

I want to back away but she has this death grip on my hands, and if I try and break away I'm gonna hurt her—physically, possibly, but I'd definitely hurt her feelings.

Ah crap, I hate feelings.

But she's still talking. About feelings. About *her* feelings for *me*.

I am in hell. I am literally in hell right now. Somebody resuscitate me because I clearly died on the field and this is my punishment for every crappy thing I've ever done.

"But I guess all I'm trying to say is, I'm happy for you," Leah continues with a sigh.

I feel a jolt of hope because her tone says she's wrapping up and maybe I can escape.

"I think I would have been heartbroken if you'd just rejected me outright, you know?" Her eyes are all wide and pleading and I find myself nodding. I don't know why.

"But the fact that you have feelings for Mara. That you two have this connection?" Her smile is small and tight, but it's the sheen of tears in her eyes that make my brain fritz out.

I am a deer in headlights.

"It's so beautiful to see you two overcome your issues and see what's been right in front of your faces all this time, you know?"

No. I don't know.

She squeezes my hands again. "I'm truly glad you and Mara are a couple, and I just wanted you to know that there are no hard feelings."

"Thank you?" It comes out as a question, and I'm not sure I'm still speaking English.

I don't know why I'm talking at all. My head is buzzing, but a little sanity returns when she lets go of my hands and backs away. "I saw Mara came to watch you practice," she continues, her eyes bright once more, but I swear this girl is crying *happy* tears.

For me.

And Mara.

Because she thinks we're a couple.

Oh crap.

I nod, because it seems to be expected.

"So it's official then?" She claps her hands together, and for no reason I can explain, I have this vivid memory of Mara doing a ridiculous dance when she won ping pong.

"What?" I ask when it's clear Leah is waiting for me to continue.

"You and Mara," she continues. "You guys are officially a couple then."

It's not a question but a confirmation and all I have to do is nod.

Which I do.

Because I am an idiot.

Her smile grows again, but she's aiming that Disney princess smile at someone just behind me. "Hey Ben, did you hear the good news? Ryan and Mara are officially a couple."

I turn to look even though I know what I'm going to see.

Oh *crap*.

Ben gives me a little nod and a halfhearted attempt at a smile. "Congratulations...I guess."

"Yeah," I say. "Thanks."

I think Leah says something else, but I don't listen, because...

Oh crap.

Mara is going to *kill* me.

SEVEN

Mara

THE PARTY TONIGHT is at Elijah's house and I'm already regretting my decision to go.

"Are you sure I look okay?" I ask for the tenth time.

Celia's climbing out of the driver's side while Addie and our friend Noelle climb out the back.

"You look hot," Noelle says.

"You look hotter," I say. Not to fish for compliments but because the tall, long-haired cheerleader truly looks freakin' phenomenal.

But she's naturally stunning, with the kind of high cheekbones, dark skin, and sharp facial features that make me feel like I'm uncooked dough. Plus, she has the curves that make her figure-hugging dress look like it was designed with her in mind. With long black hair falling in a curtain down her back, she's the picture of elegance and grace as she struts over to me in her heels.

Me? Not feeling so elegant, to be honest.

I tug at the too-short leather skirt that Celia made me wear. No one is going to confuse me with a supermodel over here, and I probably would have been a heck of a lot more comfortable wearing jeans.

But, as Celia keeps pointing out, the goal is not to be comfortable. It's to be noticed. And I am ready for Ben to notice me as something other than his gal pal from the student council.

Still, Addie looks super pretty *and* comfortable in a long, flowy maxi dress and strappy flats. Why couldn't I wear something like that?

"Seriously, Mara, any guy would have to be blind not to see your sex appeal tonight," Celia said as she links her arm through mine.

Sex appeal. Right. That's what I'm aiming for. "Are we sure he's even going to be here?"

"Most likely," Addie says. "Ben's been hanging out with Elijah a lot this summer, and it sounds like everybody's coming to this party."

Noelle tosses her hair with a wink. "Anybody who's anybody will be here."

I let out a sharp exhale and watch a blonde lock fly. Noelle is the one who insisted we curl my always wavy hair into intentional curls. The difference is real. Now it doesn't look like I just walked out of the shower and let it dry—which is totally my M.O. Now it curls just so around my shoulders.

I'll admit, between the hair and the low-key makeup Celia applied, I'm feeling...pretty. Maybe not strikingly so like Noelle, or effortlessly so like Addie, or adorably so like Celia.

But pretty. And that's enough.

Or, hopefully it will be enough to get Ben's attention tonight.

"I just hope Ryan went through with what he promised," I say as we approach the house where music is booming.

"Why wouldn't he?" Celia says. "It was just one of his jokes. It's not like he has anything to gain by letting all the girls in our class think he's off-limits."

Addie gives a cute little snort-laugh. "Yeah. He's probably hating this new relationship status as much as you are."

"Seriously," Noelle adds. "No girl with any self-respect would hook up with Ryan if they think he's taken."

I nod. This is true. But this turn in the conversation also raises questions...and a weird unsettled sensation in my belly. I turn to Noelle, trying to find the right words. *Does he randomly hook up with girls often? Is he some sort of player?*

I turn to face forward. Probably. I'd never really thought about it before but with an ego the size of his, it would make sense, right? My friends would probably know. Except for maybe Addie, they socialize more than I do.

They definitely spend way more time with Ryan outside of school than I do.

They'd know his reputation.

I start to ask and then stop myself three more times as I follow my friends around the side of the house and out into the giant yard beyond. I'm struck dumb for a moment. The yard is decked out in lights and lanterns, with music blasting from speakers. But it's the gazebo, the koi pond, and the rose gardens that really blow me away.

I mean, I always knew Elijah came from money, but I still hadn't imagined *this*.

It makes the two-bedroom apartment I share with my

mom look absurdly small, and not in a quaint and charming way.

I recognize just about everyone here from school, and except for the ones I've seen occasionally at the country club, it's the first time I'm seeing them. I am well aware of the fact that parties have been happening. Celia and Noelle keep me well informed. But with my work schedule, and the chores around the house, and the reading for school, I haven't really had much time for parties.

And so...I'm nervous.

Like, stupidly nervous considering I know these people. I *like* these people, for the most part. And for the most part, they like me. I have nothing to be nervous about. And yet, I still feel entirely out of my element.

I blame the skirt.

"Look, Ben's just over there," Noelle says.

I swat her hand when she goes to point. "I see him," I assure her. "Thank you."

I look to my friends with sheer, unadulterated panic. "I don't know if I can do this."

"There's no pressure, Mara," Addie says in a laidback voice that's as soothing as her smile. "Seriously. This isn't the last time you'll see Ben."

"Yeah," I agree. "But once we're in school, it'll be all about the student council or classes and—"

"I actually was talking about the back-to-school bonfire this weekend," she says.

"Oh." I blink in dismay at the thought of another party. But the bonfire by the lake is another senior year tradition so it's not like I'll skip it.

I glance down. But in good news, no one will expect me to wear this getup to a bonfire.

I don't think.

Celia breaks through my brooding and gives me a little shove in Ben's direction. "Go. Be brave."

Brave. Yes. Right. I can do that.

Ben's talking to Leah, who I love, and a few other girls who I'm friendly with. So good. Great. I can totally join this conversation and then start talking to Ben, maybe try to get him alone.

How do I get him alone? I should have asked Noelle before I'd walked away. I should have polled all of my friends for good topics of conversation.

Dang it. I am completely and utterly unprepared for this.

Fear makes me hesitate halfway across the lawn, but I force myself to keep going. Except, I don't get far before an arm wraps around my shoulders. I stagger in my heels before falling against a hard chest with an *oof*.

"Mara. You made it." Heat envelopes me so quickly, I don't know if it's from the sudden full-body contact, the deep, reverberating way he's said my name, or the sudden and horrific realization that the person holding me is none other than Ryan bane-of-my-existence Hunter.

I blink up at him, and for a second I'm too stunned to pull away.

Aside from that kiss, Ryan and I are not touchy-feely with one another. Not if you don't count that time I accidentally knocked his tooth out, and that one event was a pretty great indicator of the type of phys-ical interactions we would have if we were to have any.

But we don't. Not ever. Not except for that kiss.

Which is probably why my body is full-on freaking out when he grins down at me. I hate this cocky grin more than life itself, but this close and with his arm wrapped around me holding me flush against his side, it makes my heart leap and my belly clench.

Probably some sort of early-onset rage.

Yeah, that's it.

That's obviously why I can't catch my breath and why there's a cascade of heat surging through my veins and threading through my limbs.

"What are you doing?" I finally manage.

He glances around us, his cocky grin morphing into a smooth smile I don't trust for a second as he addresses someone over my head. "Hey guys. Look who made it."

I turn my head and...*no*.

My stomach drops as I see Ben, Leah, and Bianca standing there. Apparently while I'd been heading to them, they'd been coming this way.

Synchronicity, right? Must be fate.

This horrible urge to let out a nervous, hysteric laugh grips me and I turn my face to stop it. Unfortunately I turn my face toward Ryan, which makes it look like I'm burying my head against his chest. Like we're...like we're...

Oh crap, it looks like we're *cuddling*.

I push against him as he chats with Leah. Ben and Bianca aren't saying much. A quick glance shows that Bianca's too busy staring at her phone, and Ben's too busy staring...at me.

I use my elbow to nudge Ryan's ribs in an attempt to escape. I know he feels it because I can feel him flinch, and he misses a beat while telling Leah about his plans to win the scavenger hunt.

"Ha," I mutter, giving up the fight to remove myself from his side for one second. "Yeah right."

I feel Ryan's stare on the top of my head. "What does that mean?"

Leah and Ben look at me. Bianca even lifts her head, her eyes wide and expectant. Clearly she's been listening, at least, if not participating.

"Nothing," I mumble.

I glance up and Ryan's expression is hard to read, the flicker of emotion in his eyes even harder. Not that I care, because I don't.

I start to wriggle under his arm, heedless of how it might look or what kind of contortions it's doing to my tight skirt and lacy top.

Ryan leans down, close enough that I can feel his breath on my ear and it makes me shiver. "Just go with it," he murmurs.

Go with what? But before I can ask, he's talking again.

About me.

About...*us?*

"Yeah, we'll definitely be at the bonfire. Right, babe?" He looks at me, and there's a message in his eyes. An intensity that has me gaping at him with parted lips because...

"What is happening here?" I say.

He laughs like I'd said something funny, and then he leans down, burying his face in my hair and nuzzling my temple. "Will you just trust me for once? Just once."

No, I want to say. *Why should I?*

But I can't catch my breath. And my heart is racing like crazy. And...holy crap, it's happening again. My body is reacting to his scent or his pheromones or maybe just the heat from his skin.

I don't know what's causing this reaction, but it's making my legs feel like jelly. I automatically reach a hand out to catch myself against his chest so I don't slither down to the ground like a leaky balloon.

"See? Now is that so hard?" he asks.

I close my eyes as another shiver races through me and electricity darts down my back. Does he have any idea what he's doing to me when he whispers in my ear like this?

Possibly.

Okay, probably.

And that's confirmed when he leans back enough to give me the cockiest smirk I've ever seen. But then he turns his head to face the others. "Excuse us for a minute," he says as he tugs and steers until I'm walking away. "I need some alone time with my girl."

I'm walking away from Ben.

Why am I walking away from Ben? I'm supposed to be heading *toward* Ben.

I stop short when we're a few feet away, and a jolt of reason hits me upside the head. Why on earth am I walking away from Ben?

And...better question.

Why did Ryan just call me his girl?

EIGHT

Ryan

MARA'S GONNA FREAK. She's approximately three seconds away from completely losing her mind and—

"What on earth do you think you're doing?" Her voice is so high and screechy it makes me wince.

Not that I didn't see it coming. I did. I also deserve it. I deserve all the insults she can dish out, and I realize this.

However, I'd really love it if she didn't dish them out in public. That would kind of ruin everything.

I steer her away from the crowds and don't stop until we're alone beneath a tree, a speaker beside us drowning out our voices. Only then do I speak.

"Hear me out," I say in my most placating tone.

My most placating tone makes things worse. This is clear by the way her eyes get all wild and crazed as she shoves me away from her so she's no longer attached to my side.

Which is a shame, really. She felt really good pressed to my side.

"What is wrong with you?" Her eyes are still crazy big, and I can't help but notice that she's wearing eye makeup. Not as dramatic as the night we'd kissed, but it makes her eyelashes noticeable and the brown of her eyes seems...browner. Is that a thing?

Okay, fine, I don't know what the makeup has done, but it makes her eyes stand out and it's hard not to notice how pretty she is. She's always been pretty, but tonight she's...more. She's...she's...

Oh hell, she's *hot*.

And she's also still yelling at me, but I've been too caught up in studying her to hear the precise words. I get the gist, though.

I'm a jerk. I've betrayed her trust. I'm the devil incarnate. Something to that effect. I get that she's pissed. I get that I have a lot of explaining to do.

And yet, I can't make my mouth work because I'm too busy staring.

She's wearing a top that shows off everything and a skirt that should be illegal. For a long second, I can't tear my eyes away from the skirt—mainly, the place where it ends, revealing long, toned legs.

I've seen these legs often. Pretty much every day this summer. There's no reason that seeing them now should make me drool, but there's definitely a saliva issue happening here.

I blame the kiss. Because that's the only difference between then and now.

Then, I didn't know how good it felt to hold her in my arms. Now, all I know for certain is that I want to kiss her again more than I've ever wanted anything.

This is...not good.

"Are you even listening to me?" she asks with a huff of exasperation.

No. Not really. I clear my throat. "If you'd give me one second to explain, you'll see that this is not my fault."

She tilts her head and looks up at me. It's a holier than thou sort of look that should annoy the crap out of me, but right now it brings up thoughts of sexy librarians, and...

This is not helping the saliva issue.

"Not your fault?" She overenunciates to make her point. "Not. Your. *Fault?*"

I wince. Okay, yeah. Point taken.

"All of this is your fault," she says in a rush of flailing hands. "All of it. You bullied me into kissing you—"

"Bullied?" I interrupt. I shake my head. "No. No way. Goaded, maybe. Egged you on? Yeah, fine. But you kissed me, Mara, and I didn't exactly hear any complaints."

She stares at me with wide eyes and parted lips.

No one has to tell me that this was the wrong approach. I hurry on before she has a chance to rally. "I will admit that the comment on that photo was my fault—"

"Oh, you'll admit to that? How very good of you."

"Your sarcasm is duly noted," I say. "However, what matters now isn't about who's at fault—"

"You," she says. "*You* are at fault."

I hold my hands up in surrender. "*What matters now* is how we handle this from here on out."

"Handle what?" Her voice rises as she looks past me, no doubt to Ben. "You were supposed to handle this yesterday."

"And I did—"

"This is how you handled it?" Her brows are arched high in disbelief.

I sigh. "What I mean is, I'd started to handle it—"

"Oh, this should be good." She crosses her arms, and now it takes all of my willpower to keep from dropping my gaze to check out the cleavage she's unintentionally showing off.

"But then Leah happened," I say.

I'm not the most well-spoken guy to begin with—but add cleavage and thighs to the mix and I am a bumbling fool. I can't blame her for staring at me in disbelief before repeating my words like she's trying to decipher them.

"Then Leah happened," she says slowly. "Am I supposed to know what that means?"

I glance over toward Leah and Ben with a sigh. "The poor kid's had a crush on me for years."

"That doesn't make her a poor kid," Mara says. "More like a delusional moron." The moment the words come out she winces with regret. "I didn't mean that. I like Leah. I was trying to offend you, not her."

A smile tugs at my lips, and it's a struggle not to laugh. I'm pretty sure me laughing would end in my demise, so I manage to hold it in. "Understood."

"So Leah likes you," Mara says with a shrug. "What does that have to do with anything?"

Now it's my turn to wince. "She got the wrong idea about us—"

"No, you gave people the wrong idea," she says.

I roll my eyes. "Fine. Whatever. But, Mara, you should have seen the way she looked at me when she kept telling me how happy she was for us."

Mara narrows her gaze. "You're insane. You know that, right?"

"You wouldn't be saying that if you'd been there. You wouldn't have been able to tell her the truth either."

She scoffs. "Please. Give me some credit. You might not be able to do the hard things, but I don't have that problem."

She's pissed. I get that. But something in her words is more heated than I like. More...personal. It feels like a dig in more ways than one. Like she's not just talking about Leah. It brings me right back to that moment with Ben, Leah, and Bianca when she got all sarcastic about me winning the scavenger hunt.

She hadn't outright insulted me, but I could feel her derision then just like I do now. She's judging me. Again. Like always. But tonight, it stings more than usual.

Can I blame the kiss for this change too?

Maybe. Maybe not.

Maybe I've just reached my limit of Mara's judgy glares.

"What is that supposed to mean?" I snap.

Her eyes widen in surprise, but she doesn't back down. I should have known she wouldn't. She tilts her head to the side and purses her lips like she's debating what she's going to say.

I find myself tensing. Bracing for impact, even though I'm fully prepared to laugh off whatever new criticism she throws my way.

She shrugs. "You're not good at doing difficult things, that's all."

"*What?*" I spit the word out in disbelief.

She shrugs again, and I hate that freakin' shrug. "That's why I know you won't win the scavenger hunt, and it's why you couldn't just tell Leah the truth yesterday." She glares. "Or Ben, apparently."

"He overheard," I start to protest. But I stop short because that's not the point. That's definitely not the comment that makes me want to scream bloody murder right now. "How can you say I don't do difficult things? Do you know how I spent my day yesterday?" I don't give her a chance to respond. "I had my ass handed to me all day long by my coach. And do you know what I did this morning?" I lean in toward her. "I got up and did it all over again."

Her gaze is unflinching, her expression unimpressed. "That's not what I was referring to."

I don't want to ask. I don't even want to be having this conversation. And I certainly don't want to be feeling...this. Whatever this is.

I'm used to Mara being a condescending know-it-all, but I'm not used to it getting to me like this. I've never felt like I've taken a kick to the gut or like someone's reached inside and twisted my insides into a knot.

I'd love to blame the kiss, but this is not that. This is not a physical reaction to her body or her closeness. This is her words gnawing at my gut. It's a lifetime of her judgmental catty comments all coming together at once, because...this?

This is her problem with me.

I can see it in her eyes and it makes me want to freakin tear down the sky with my bare hands. She's looking right into me, right through me—and she hates what she sees.

"So let me get this straight." Despite what's going on inside, my voice is hard, my stance wide, and my arms crossed in a defensive pose. "Are you calling me a wuss?"

Her lip curves slightly in a sneer. "I didn't say that."

"But it's what you mean," I shoot back.

"No, it's just..." She exhales loudly and tosses her hands up in the air, like I'm the exhausting one here. "You want to know what I think? Fine. I think you've gone your entire life without having to take any responsibility. Without having to man up."

I glare at her as her words hit my skin like barbed wire. "You're insane."

"Am I?" Her cheeks are getting pink now as she gets worked up. "You don't take responsibility, and you don't take chances. That's what I think."

"What are you even talking about?" I'm practically shouting now, and thank goodness for the speakers because if people could hear us, we'd be putting on a show. We're probably already putting on a show if anyone is looking our way.

But I don't care. I'm barely aware of the party going on around us as I wait for her to continue. Her accusations are like a car crash. It's painful. It's horrible. I don't want to see the casualties. But I can't look away either. Some sick masochistic part of me wants to hear this. All of it.

I *need* to hear it.

"You know what? Forget it." She's shaking her head. "I shouldn't have said anything."

"Oh no," I say. "You can't just stop like that." I see the guilt in her eyes before she looks away and that makes it even worse. If I thought for one second she was only saying this crap to hurt me or to make me feel bad, I could laugh it off. But she looks freakin' *guilty*. Like she's honestly sorry.

Like she's honestly telling me the truth.

"Nope," I say when she starts to walk away. "You don't get to just walk away from this. Not until you're done."

"It's not my place to psychoanalyze you," she mutters, her gaze on the ground somewhere behind me rather than meeting my eyes.

"But you have. And I wonder why that is, Mara. Hmm?" I'm taunting her and I know it.

Her gaze flashes back to mine, and there's a flicker of fire there. "What's that supposed to mean?"

"Considering how little you think of me, you seem to spend an inordinate amount of time thinking *about* me."

Her brows knit together, but she doesn't protest.

"So finish," I say, crossing my arms again and glaring down at her. "Finish what you started."

"Fine." Her chin lifts and her eyes meet mine. "You don't do anything unless you know you can win."

I blink. My mind races to come up with proof that she's wrong, and...I draw a blank.

Is she right? I don't know. All I know is, I can't come up with a single argument to fight back, and I don't want to think about it anymore. Not now while she's watching me, looking at me like she knows me better than I know myself. So I curve my lips up into a smirk and lighten my tone. "You make that sound like a bad thing."

She huffs, and I swear I see disappointment in her eyes. "I don't even know why we're talking about this. None of this matters." She points toward the crowd. "You need to go fix this."

And now we're back to Ben. That's all she's worried about. She just reached in, messed with my insides, and all she cares about is getting with some guy she barely knows. But it's not just about Ben, and she doesn't seem to get that.

"Do you really want to break Leah's heart?" I ask.

"Oh please. Your ego is so out of control." She rolls her eyes. "Leah's heart is not going to be broken just because the great Ryan Hunter doesn't return her feelings."

Ugh. There's the F-word again. *Feelings*. I turn to glance over at the girl we're talking about and see her looking right back. And she's not the only one.

"Don't look now, but your lover boy is watching," I say.

"What?" she snaps. "What are you talking about?"

"Look to your right," I say. "And try to be cool about it, yeah?"

She's not cool about it. Not at all. She whips her head

around and no doubt makes eye contact with Ben the Bore. Her gaze comes swinging back to meet mine and her eyes are wide with surprise. "Oh," she says.

Clearly she saw it too.

Ben isn't just looking our way. He's staring. Maybe even glaring.

"Maybe they know we're fighting," Mara says. She looks deep in thought as she nibbles on her lower lip.

Crap. The outfit is bad enough. The makeup is not helping. But now nibbling?

Is she trying to kill me?

I look away in disgust—not with her, but with myself. The girl just tore me a new one. She basically smashed my pride, and I know for a fact I'll be stewing over her little personality assessment for way longer than I'll ever admit.

And yet, despite all that, I still want to kiss the hell out of her. And I don't want it to be a dare, and I don't want an audience...and I don't want it to end.

So, what the hell does this say about me?

The answer's obvious.

I am definitely a masochist.

NINE

Mara

RYAN CHASES after me when I walk away.

"You're not really going to do this," he says.

He sounds so sure of himself.

Jackass.

"Why wouldn't I?" These stupid heels are making it hard to storm off. My dramatic and sudden exit from the conversation is ruined as I totter precariously with each slow step. I want to run—not because I'm so desperate to confront Leah and Ben to tell them the truth, but because I hate myself right now.

I know I can't run away from myself, but would a minute alone to gather my thoughts be asking for too much?

I shouldn't have said all that to Ryan. It was mean. Just straight up mean.

Was it the truth? Yeah. Maybe. At least, it's my take on Ryan. But it definitely wasn't my place to spout off like that. Guilt is nagging at me, and it's hard to say how much of that guilt is because of what I'd said to Ryan. Because I'm also feeling plenty guilty about the fact that, for a second there, I was a little tempted to go along with this stupid ruse.

Ben really did look jealous.

I hate that I loved that.

Basically, I'm just being eaten alive by guilt on all fronts, and I'd kill for a few seconds to sort through my thoughts. But Ryan is hounding my every step, telling me to slow down. To reconsider. Asking me what I'm even going to say.

That does give me pause, and he exhales loudly in relief when I stop halfway to Ben and Leah. Bianca's left them and they're talking to each other, blissfully unaware that Ryan and I are big fat liars.

Well, Ryan's a liar. I'm just guilty by association. Unless I set this right. Which I will do. Just as soon as I figure out how. I mean, one doesn't just walk up to people at a party and confess that they're not really dating. *Ryan only told you that because he felt sorry for you.*

I cringe.

Yeah, no. That's not going to work.

"Not so gung ho *now*, are we?" Ryan's way too pleased with himself as he rocks back on his heels and watches me think.

There are people all around us, and yet they give us space. That's a Ryan thing. He's a big guy, and he takes up space in a way that's hard to describe. His whole demeanor is like the confidence version of manspreading.

Normally it's one of the many things about him that drives me nuts. But right now, I'm kind of grateful for it because he buys me some space. Granted, *he's* in my space, but if he can just keep quiet for more than two seconds, I'll take it.

"Having a change of heart?" he asks.

Apparently two seconds of silence is too much to ask from this one. I shoot him glare and he chuckles.

"What is it? You having second thoughts about ripping poor Leah's heart out?" he continues. "That's a good thing, Mara, it means you're not on track to being a supervillain."

I roll my eyes and shake my head as I fight this stupid urge to laugh.

"Some people refer to you as Maleficent, but I always stick up for you," he continues. "*No, no*, I always say. She's not *that* evil."

A choking sound escapes before I can stop it, and then I'm clapping a hand over my mouth to stop a laugh.

I will *not* laugh at this jerk's teasing. It will only encourage him.

But it's too late. He's heard my snicker and he's grinning in triumph. The sight makes my chest tighten because...guilt.

I just reamed him out and now he's smiling at me? He shouldn't be teasing and making me laugh because I am the worst. I mean, I might hate the guy, but no one deserves to hear their fatal flaws spelled out like that.

I look up again, with my hand over my mouth, and that tightness in my chest grows because also...hotness. He is so hot right now I can't even breathe.

He's a handsome guy. He always has been, he likely always will be. But smiling like this? Not a smirk but a full-blown grin that has his blue eyes sparkling with laughter and little dimples showing at the corners of his mouth.

Yeah, I officially can't draw in air.

"Seriously, Mara, look at her." He nods toward Leah. "You can't tell her the brutal truth."

Not like I'd just done to him, he means.

"I don't think lying helps anyone," I say.

"I don't know," he says slowly. "I think there's a difference between calling someone on their BS and letting someone believe a lie so they don't get hurt."

Are we still talking about Leah right now? I look away because I'm not sure.

"I'll tell you what," he starts.

Something about the change in his voice makes me tense as I look up at him. He sounds like he's plotting something, and that's never a good thing. His hands are tucked in the jeans of his pockets as he considers me in turn.

"I'll go over there with you," he says. "And if you can actually bring yourself to tell Leah the truth, then I'll have your back."

I arch a brow. He's surprisingly serious and a voice in the back of my brain is asking if this offer has anything to do with what I just said to him before.

If maybe he's stepping up because I called him out.

I don't have much of a chance to decide before I'm put to the test. Leah and Ben join us. Ben stands right next to me. So close our arms are brushing.

"You okay?" he asks. The concern in his voice is sweet.

I nod. "Yeah, we're fine, just—"

"A new couple disagreement, right?" Leah finishes. She flashes Ben a triumphant smile. "See? I told you they'd work it out."

I feel Ryan's eyes on me. I'm pretty sure I can feel his smirk, if that's possible. I clear my throat. "Yeah, well, that's the thing—"

I stop when I'm tackled. Leah's arms are around my neck and she's holding me tight. Her voice is an excited squeal. "You guys are so cute together."

"Oh, uh…" I meet Ryan's gaze over her shoulder and he arches his brows in a silent challenge.

He's enjoying my discomfort, the jerk.

I pat her back and try to wiggle out of her embrace. "Thanks, Leah, but actually—"

"I told Ryan, but I wanted to tell you too," she says, talking right over me in a barrage of words. "I thought I'd be crushed to see Ryan with another girl." She gives me a sheepish grin. "I had a crush."

I open my mouth, but she's not done.

"So, you know, I thought I'd be really upset, right? But the thing is, seeing you two together made it feel okay that he didn't feel the same way as me, you know? Because he couldn't, obviously. Because he had feelings for you." Her eyes are wide and expectant, her smile so bright it hurts to look at. "You know?"

After this second 'you know?' she actually pauses like she's waiting for an answer.

I open my mouth and a sound escapes. "Uhhh…"

"Of course you know," she says with a shake of her head like she's said something silly. "I was just telling Ben that I should have seen it coming, I really should have." She turns her beaming smile from me to Ryan and then back again. "This explains so much."

My mouth reflexively returns her smile like it's on autopilot, but it feels way too strained. "Does it?"

This is enough to set Leah off again, but my brain is still fixed on what she'd just said. She'd be crushed if he didn't like her for no good reason.

I don't get it. But then again, I don't get why she likes Ryan in the first place.

I glance over at Ben, like he might be able to sense my dilemma and come to my rescue. He just gives me a little smile. A shared look of understanding that we're listening to an excessively enthusiastic creature go on at great length about my supposed new relationship.

My face is starting to hurt from fake smiling.

I look to Ryan, and that's a mistake. He's not smiling and he doesn't look smug. He's watching me and his expression is intense. His gaze is fierce and hot and—

I wish I knew what he's thinking.

Whatever it is, he seems to come to some decision as his gaze meets mine because he shifts to stand closer to me and he glides a hand over my back and around my waist. Just like an actual boyfriend might.

My lungs are not working right. I'm taking these weird, shallow gulps of air as every part of my brain fixates on the feel of his big, warm palm that's clamped onto my waist. The lace top rides up a bit and his hand is directly on my skin.

I'm pretty sure I'm burning up where he's touching me, but that's nothing compared to the singeing heat in my belly when he looks down at me. "What do you think, babe?"

I swallow. I have no idea what they were just talking about, but it doesn't matter because that's not what he's asking.

I know what he's really asking. Am I in or out? Am I going to go along with this lie or am I going to open my mouth and break poor Leah's heart?

I nod and his lips quirk up on one side. But it's not a smirk, just a knowing smile. And then he turns to the others and makes our excuses. He says something about getting me a drink, even though he knows very well I don't drink.

But I smile and nod and let him lead me away. It's not until they're well behind me and we're swallowed up by a crowd that I let out a long breath. But my relief is short lived because...the people in this crowd? They're staring at me. No, at *us*.

"Why is everyone smiling at us?" I ask.

He leans down to talk closer to my ear as we pass a speaker and a handful of girls who are dancing like they're at a club in LA and not in a suburban backyard. "Everyone loves a good love story," he says.

I pull my head back to meet his gaze. "Wait, you think..." I look around us and it's alarming how much attention we're drawing. I stumble in my heels, but Ryan's hand at my waist holds me steady. "They all think we're really in love?"

"It's a small school, Mara. You know how it is."

"Right," I say. But I don't. I really don't. I have been the center of attention before. Mainly at school assemblies when I address the crowd on behalf of the student council, or during softball season and we win a game.

I've never once been the girl that people gossip about though. One typically has to have a life to be the subject of gossip, and my life has been tame to the point of dull for as long as I can remember.

My mind flashes to the scavenger hunt. To the decision I'd made that this year will be different. Everyone thinking Ryan Hunter is my boyfriend? This is definitely different.

So that's something. Right?

I glance up at him. This is not necessarily a *good* some-thing, but it's something. But even as I think it, my heart starts to race and my brain...? Forget it. My brain is working so fast I can't keep up with all the thoughts.

Doubts, mainly.

"Hey, Mara?" Ryan's voice has got that laid back tone I can't stand. Although, in all honesty, right this second—it's a little comforting.

"Yes?" I say.

"Are you going to freak out now?" His voice is so calm, so pleasant.

"Yes."

"That's what I thought." He steers us toward the side of the house.

"Where are we going?" I ask.

"Somewhere you can freak out in peace."

I'm equally annoyed and relieved. I do want to freak out in peace, but I'd rather not freak out at all. And if I have to freak out, he should be freaking out right alongside me.

"How are you so calm about this?" I say. "We're going to have to lie to everyone we know."

He arches his brows when he looks down at me. "First, I'm a good liar."

"That's really not something you should brag about."

He ignores that. "And second..." He stops when we reach the side of his car which is parked by the curb out front. "Who says we'll be lying?"

"Wait, what?" But then my confusion turns to panic as he drops his arm and turns away. "Where are you going?"

He can't just leave me like this. Not until he explains how we're going to do this and—

Gah! I don't even recognize myself right now. I'm needy and pleading, and when he turns to stare at me, it's clear he's equally confused.

He nods toward the driver's side. "I didn't think you'd want to sit in my lap." A smirk tugs at his lips. "But if you'd rather we share—"

"Go to your side." I point as I say it and ignore his low chuckle.

I'm *so* glad I can be a source of amusement to him right now.

I slide into the car's passenger seat as he climbs in the driver's side, and when both doors shut and the lights dim to darkness, it's...nice.

It's a relief, at least.

The music from the party is just a dull beat, and the curious stares are out of sight. I drop my head back against the headrest, and we sit in silence for a full minute.

"Better?" he asks softly.

I roll my head to the side so I can see him. The car is dark, but a streetlight overheard casts enough light that I can make out his features. I can see his eyes.

He's not laughing at me.

For once, he's not laughing at me.

I take a deep breath. My mind is able to function again, and I'm not sure that's entirely a good thing. I have questions. And I'm seriously doubting this decision. "This was a mistake," I say.

He laughs. "Too late to turn back, Sunshine."

I try to shoot him a glare, but I don't really have the energy. All of my brain cells are too busy trying to figure out all the ways this can, and most likely will, go wrong. "We need to set some ground rules."

"Of course we do." His voice drips with sarcasm.

"I'm serious." I shift in my seat to face him.

"Of course you are." There's that tone again.

"Will you cut that out?" I snap.

He grins. "All right, fine. What're the ground rules?"

"We need an end date," I say.

"Easy. Leah always heads back home shortly after we start school—"

"Yeah," I say. I remember this from past summers. "Her school starts up a couple weeks after ours, right?"

"Exactly. So all we have to do is keep this up until she's

gone. That way, she doesn't get hurt. We tell everyone we tried the couple thing and failed—"

"And you don't have to worry about rejecting Leah," I say. "Until next summer, at least."

His wince makes me smile. It's kind of nice seeing this side of Ryan. The part that actually cares about someone else's feelings. He may have gone about sparing her feelings all wrong, but the fact that he's going to this trouble is oddly endearing.

Not that I'll ever admit that aloud.

"Okay, so a couple of weeks," I say. "That's not too bad. I think I can manage that."

He gives a little snort of amusement. "You can handle dating me for a couple weeks? I'm so honored."

His point is taken. There are a whole lot of girls who'd kill to be in my position, of this I have no doubt. But I am not one of those girls.

"What other ground rules?" He taps his fingers on the steering wheel, and my previously active brain goes blank. For a second I become acutely aware of the fact that we are alone. Together.

Together and alone.

"Um..." I say.

He arches his brows in a prompt.

"Scavenger hunt," I say.

He blinks. "Pardon?"

I shift again to face him fully as the idea develops into fruition. Yeah. This is good. My heart starts to pound. "I'm basically just covering for your lies here, buddy, so in exchange you have to help me win the scavenger hunt."

He shrugs. "Yeah. Okay, fine." He looks at me like he's waiting for me to say something else. Like he's waiting for something in particular.

It hits me upside the head like a smack. "Ben!" I say.

He laughs. "And there it is."

I point a finger right at his nose. "You help me get Ben."

"That's a given." He says this so easily, it doesn't sit right. "Anything else?" he asks.

I try and think, but my thoughts are hung up on that one strange comment from earlier. "What did you mean before when you said we wouldn't necessarily be lying."

He leans forward slightly and I get a whiff of boy. I don't know whether it's his soap or his pheromones or what, but it's all guy and it's all consuming. I swallow hard and watch his lips as they curve up so very slowly.

"You know you're a terrible liar, right?" he asks.

I nod. This is not news to anyone.

He shrugs. "Then the easiest way to get through this is to make this real. *Short term*," he says pointedly—as if I'm going to get ideas. "But real."

"But...But..." I have lost the ability to speak. "What does that mean?"

"We may have gotten into this because of a lie, but if I know you—" He fixes me with a meaningful look. "And I *do*. Then the only way you'll survive without dying of guilt or shouting the truth out under duress is to make it real."

"W-why? How?" I open my mouth again but the only words I can think of are more one-syllable questions. I close it and try to think of anything else to say. All I come up with is, "I don't understand."

He leans back in his seat and the look he gives me is so familiar it puts me at ease even as it annoys the crap out of me.

It's condescending and smirky, and I hate it.

"You're making too big of a deal out of it, Mara. People hook up all the time for all sorts of reasons."

I kind of want to smack him.

"What's our reason?" I ask. I'll admit it. I'm intrigued by his logic.

He reaches out and tugs one of the curls that's still lying perfectly against my shoulder. "Maybe we're curious," he says slowly. "Maybe we kissed once, on a dare, and there was chemistry there."

My breath catches in my throat when his gaze falls to my lips and stays there. His voice is low and soft, and it's weaving around me like a hypnotic melody.

"Maybe that kiss left us both curious," he says. "Maybe that one kiss gave us ideas."

His gaze lifts to meet mine and I blink. I know what he's doing. Of course I do. He's writing our story. A lie.

But a lie that feels real.

A lie that might be real. If we let it.

"So we agree to try dating. Just for a little. Just to see if there's an actual connection there or if it was just physical compatibility."

My mouth is dry, and I swear I can feel his voice in my belly, in my chest. The low rumble is making my insides tremble. "I suppose that's...feasible."

He laughs softly, dropping his head and breaking the moment. When he lifts his head, his gaze isn't nearly as serious, and he's wearing a smile I've seen a million times, just never aimed at me. "So what do you say, Mara? Do you want to be my temporary girlfriend?"

I sigh as my insides settle, and my mind stops whirring and lands on one answer. "I guess so."

"Wow," he deadpans. "Your enthusiasm is overwhelming."

"I think your ego can handle it." I crack a smile. "But

you're right. It's too late now, so we might as well make the best of it."

He nods. "Right. We'll...make the best of it."

The way he hesitates gives me pause, but I don't question it. Instead, I turn to him once more with another question. "So, what's next?"

TEN

Ryan

DID I invite Mara to the lake with me and my buddies the next day just so I could ogle her in a swimsuit some more?

No. But it's a great bonus.

"Wow, when did Mara Loman become such a hottie?" Elijah asks.

I glance over and then frown when I see that I'm not the only one ogling. All of my buddies are too, and that is not okay. "Hey, eyes off my girl."

I'm ignored by all of the guys who are sprawled out around the picnic table where we've made camp for the day. It's a gorgeous sunny afternoon, and one of the last days before school so we are definitely not alone in this plan to enjoy the lake.

Mara had to work at the club this morning, but when her shift was over, I picked her up and we met our friends here. She's lying out on a blanket with her friends Celia and Addie now, but showing up together was statement enough.

It's all anyone's been talking about.

"My question is, since when have you been into her?" Heath asks.

I shrug. I don't really want to lie to my friends, but I don't care to explain either.

"Since forever, obviously," Pamela says. Her tone is so knowing, and the coy look she sends me makes me flinch. She's the only one of the girls who's hanging out with us, and she's plastered to Heath's side like a second skin.

My guess is this is why Mara's friends are off on their own. Celia's probably not dying to hang out with her crush and her crush's girlfriend.

And yes, I totally know about Celia's thing for Heath. I'm pretty sure Heath's the only one who hasn't figured out that the reason the outgoing sweetheart clams up around him is because she gets nervous.

At least, I assume that's the case.

"Didn't you see them at the country club party?" Pamela continues. "That kiss was so hot."

I look away, back to Mara. There are few things I'd like to do less than recount one of the more epic moments of my life with Pamela the shallow soul sucker.

Mara sits up and says something to her friends. She's smiling, laughing. This is the side of Mara I almost never get to see. At school and at the pool, she's all work mode all the time. And when it comes to me in particular, I can't do anything right.

"I always thought you two hated each other." That comes from Toby at the far end of the table near the drinks. He sounds confused.

Rightfully so.

"Yeah, well." I shrug. "Things change."

And I want to change the topic. Even better, the

company. I love my friends, but I'm tired of watching Mara. I want to know what they're talking about, what has her laughing so much.

Does she always laugh this much when she's with her friends?

Is she always so smiley when I'm not around?

The questions leave me disgruntled and I rethink my idea of going over to join her. The last thing I want to see is her face fall when I sit down beside her. But then, I don't have to go to them because she's getting up, adjusting her swimsuit which hides absolutely nothing of that glorious body of hers, and she's heading our way.

She's walking over to *me*.

"Seriously, how have I not noticed how hot she's gotten?" Elijah wonders aloud.

"Stop noticing," I growl.

This makes Pamela laugh, and even Heath drops his head to snicker at my expense.

"What?" I snap.

Heath reaches for a water bottle. "Never thought you'd be the jealous boyfriend type."

"I'm not her—" I stop short.

Oh crap. My head is so not in the game if I just came that close to spilling our little secret. I clamp my mouth shut and turn my gaze and nearly have a heart attack at the sight before me.

Don't get me wrong. I've known all summer that I find her attractive. I've known way longer than that that she's hot. Maybe not in an over-the-top way. She's never tried to call attention to her looks. But I've always known.

The only reason these other guys are noticing now is because they're finally looking.

I don't have to glance over to the dock where Ben's

hanging out with some of his friends to know that he's looking too.

What is that? Why is it that people suddenly wake up and see what's right in front of them after someone else spots it first? Is it a law of nature or something or—

"Am I interrupting?" Mara sidles up next to me with a smile that steals the air from my lungs.

It's the smile she wears for her friends. It's a real smile. And she's looking at me.

"You guys having fun?" I ask.

She nods. "Yeah. I am."

I'm probably the only one who understands the surprise that underlies her tone.

"I'm glad the country club cut the pool hours this week so we can enjoy it," she says.

"Speaking of the country club," Pamela cuts in loudly before I can respond, and all eyes are on us. "We were just talking about how you two finally got together."

"Oh yeah?" Mara tries to sound calm and collected, but she fails. And her cheeks are already turning a bright pink.

"That kiss was epic," Pamela continues. She leans forward and uses this tone of voice like she and Mara are alone and sharing some girl talk. "Tell me honestly, though. You've had a thing for Ryan all along, right? I mean how could you not."

"Pamela," Heath mutters in warning. He gives Mara an apologetic little wince. He and Mara are similar in the sense that neither would be cool with their personal lives being public knowledge or a topic of gossip.

I look from Heath to Mara and back again, this time giving Heath a scowl. He can be nice to Mara...but not too nice. He'd better not have started noticing how hot Mara is too, or I might have to hurt someone.

Mara's voice cuts into this weird new anger. It's not jealousy, obviously.

But it's close.

It's disturbingly close.

"I definitely have not been harboring a great love for Ryan." Mara sounds like she's on the verge of laughter. I must have missed some of this exchange because Mara's gone from embarrassed to amused.

How hilarious to think she might have a thing for me, right?

Ha ha. Super funny.

"As one of her oldest friends, I can confirm this." Celia's come over to join us, and I see Addie on her way as well. A few of the guys from my crew are playing beach volleyball, along with some girls—including Leah, I see. So there's room for Mara's friends at our spot.

Celia sits on the far end of the table, the farthest she can get from Heath, and Addie slides in between Heath and Elijah.

And now that everyone's found a topic they all can share in, they're off and running.

Unfortunately for me, the topic is how much Mara and I have fought over the years. She's still standing next to me, laughing and cringing a bit as our friends reminisce about the early days of our feuding. We'd been far more boisterous and way less sarcastic in our barbs back then.

As if she's reading my mind, Mara murmurs, "Ah the good old days when fighting was simple."

I laugh, and she glances over like she's surprised to see me there. Or maybe she just hadn't expected me to hear her.

I snag her hand and tug. She's perched on my knee, and at first, she looks more tense and awkward than I can stand, but after a few seconds and several deep breaths, she relaxes into it.

My hands are at her waist, and her skin is crazy warm where I'm touching her. Neither of us speak for a while, and I wonder if she's lost the ability to pay attention too. Who can listen to old childhood stories when she's half naked and in my lap?

I feel it when she tenses at something Addie says. That causes me to pay attention, and I realize they're talking about *it*. The great debate that launched our long-standing rivalry.

"But seriously," Addie says. "I can't believe they let a fight that started when they were eight years old get so out of control."

"What happened?" Pamela asks.

Mara casts me a quick look over her shoulder, and now I'm tensing too. No. No way. There's no way we're rehashing this again.

"He cheated," she says. "It was at Molly Harper's birthday party and it was a swim race, and Ryan cheated."

I open my mouth to argue, but what's the point? Also, we're supposed to be dating, right? So instead of arguing, I tug her back into my arms, wrapping my arms around her so quickly she squeaks. I give a playful growl, and to my surprise, she laughs as she fights back.

Everyone's watching, and part of me thinks this is just for show...but a part of me knows Mara better than that. Enough to know she can't act to save her life. But when her wriggling doesn't work and I'm laughing too as I hold her tight to my chest, she surprises the crap out of me by turning her head and planting a quick kiss on my cheek.

I let go instantly, and she crows in victory.

Competitive little witch.

But I'm grinning as I touch my cheek. It's so stupid. It was just a little peck on the cheek.

But there's something inside me that's warm and glowing at the simple, sweet show of affection, and it's taking over my chest.

She shifts so she's facing me, and I am painfully aware that everyone is watching us.

That's what this is all about. I get that. But it's also a pain in the butt because I am craving a minute alone with her. Just one.

"You know what I think we need?" Her eyes are dancing with mischief.

This is rare. It's so freakin' rare for me to see this. A playful Mara? I'd started to think she didn't exist. I run my hands over the soft skin of her back. "What's that?"

She leans in close, and my heart pounds like crazy as she whispers, "A do-over."

I blink. "What?"

She leans back again, her voice returning to a normal volume as everyone listens in. "A do-over." She shrugs. "You. Me. A race." She narrows her eyes in a threat—now this is a side of Mara I know well. "No cheating."

I open my mouth to argue, but our friends are into this idea. They're laughing and coming up with the rules for this race.

I sigh as I meet her smug gaze.

"Oh, you are going down," I say in a low tone just for her. But I'm teasing, and she knows it. She doesn't get all defensive like she normally would, she just shrugs.

"We'll see."

"To the island," Elijah announces. No surprise that Elijah is the one to come up with the challenge—or that it's a dangerous one, at that.

"That's too far," Addie says.

Mara and I exchange a glance before we both follow where the others are looking—at the island in the middle of the lake. It's not actually an island. It's more like a peninsula, but the land leading to it is rocky and government owned, so the only real way to get there is by boat or swimming.

"I can do it," Mara says with so much swagger I feel a jolt of desire all over again. She arches a brow at me, and there's no way I'm saying no to this challenge.

Is this going to change anything? No. Is it going to rewrite history? Absolutely not.

Is it a bad idea?

I'm pretty sure it is. But she's issuing a challenge with that look of hers, and at this moment, nothing has ever seemed hotter. I meet her gaze with a grin. "Let's do this."

ELEVEN

Mara

HE LETS ME WIN.

The jerk *lets me win.*

I climb up onto the island and plant my hands on my hips as he follows just behind me.

"Why did you do that?" I ask.

He's grinning as he steps out of the lake, water dripping down his chest like he's posing on the set of some cologne photoshoot or something.

Meanwhile, I'm all winded and bent over trying to catch my breath. "You let me win."

"I did nothing of the sort," he says. He looks offended, but his grin's barely faded and he's walking toward me with too much swagger for someone who just lost.

"Then how are you not even a little out of breath?" I ask.

The wind whips around me, and for the first time I

really notice how alone we are on this little strip of land that's covered with nothing but tree branches and rocks.

It's oddly freeing to be here alone with him. For the first time all day I don't have to monitor what I say or fear that I'll slip up and accidentally break Leah's heart.

I drop down onto my butt in the rocky sand and he sinks down beside me.

He's still way too smug, but I'm losing some of my fire. Probably because I've thoroughly exhausted myself with that swim.

I'm a good swimmer, but it's not like I'm on the swim team or anything. It's been ages since I've swum so fast or so far. I glance over at a totally relaxed Ryan who's leaning back and soaking up the sun.

Or...he *was* in the sun. As I watch, a shadow falls over us. I look up and groan. "Oh no."

"Bad timing," he says. He sees it too, the storm cloud rolling overhead. He leans over and nudges my shoulder with his. "It'll pass quickly, we just have to wait it out."

I nod. I wasn't really all that worried, but his attempt to comfort me is kinda sweet. I watch as the wind makes the water before us get choppier and choppier. "Until it passes..." I start.

"You're stuck with me." He looks way too pleased with himself. As if he single handedly brought on the late afternoon showers just to mess with me.

"Maybe *you're* stuck with *me*," I say.

He shakes his head with a chuckle. "Always have to have the last word, don't you?"

I bite my tongue to keep from having the last word again. Because the answer is yes, I do like to have the last word. And I'm well aware that my competitive nature can be a bit...extreme. Especially around a certain someone who may or may not have the most ridiculous abs known to man.

I look away quickly before I'm caught staring.

Instead, I stare down at my toes as I dig my feet into the sand. I'd hoped the swim would clear my head, but in this silence, I'm right back to stewing over the stories our friends were telling just moments before. I've always known my reactions to Ryan and his teasing have been on the extreme side, but hearing all those stories from my friend's point of view was humbling. They left me with this gross feeling in my gut. Shame, maybe?

Embarrassment, definitely.

I've always prided myself on being the mature one. The responsible one. But hearing those stories...well, nothing about my actions sounded mature. Not in the least.

"What?" Ryan says suddenly beside me. He's sprawled out on his back, his head resting on his hands as he waits for the rain to hit us. He rolls his head to the side to meet my gaze. "What're you angsting about over there?"

"I'm not angsting." But I am. I don't know why I'm even trying to lie at this point. I'm not good at it, and apparently Ryan can see through my lies better than anyone. I take a deep breath and let it out slowly. "I was just thinking of those stories our friends were telling. About us. About our past."

He's silent for a beat. "What about them?"

I bite my lip as my stomach roils. Am I really about to do this? "I'm sorry for my part in our..." I wave a hand. "Feud."

He's silent for so long I start to shift uncomfortably on the sand. When I glance over, I see him watching me with this little smile that I don't understand.

"What?" I say.

His smile grows. "How much did it hurt you to say that?"

I open my mouth, ready to say something defensive. But I catch the glimmer of laughter in his eyes, and rather than snap back, I laugh under my breath, turning back to look at the waves on the lake. "A lot," I say. "It did *not* feel good."

He's laughing as he sits up. "Well, if it helps, I'm sorry too. For my part."

He's slightly less awkward about it than I was, but I can see how hard it was for him to say those words too, and I can't help it. I crack up.

His eyes widen in surprise at my laughter, but then he joins me, and for a moment, we just sit there laughing over how ridiculous we are. I turn to him a second later. "Why did you let me win?"

He shrugs. "It means more to you than it does to me."

"Well, that's because—" I stop short when his brows hitch up slightly. It's not much, but I feel called out for my overly defensive tone. I relent with a sigh. "I just don't like when people cheat."

A muscle in his jaw twitches, and I just know he's trying not to laugh. "Yeah. I've come to understand that over the years."

Now my lips are twitching too as I shrug. "The fact that I still get worked up over something that happened when we were eight is beyond ridiculous. I know this, it's just..."

I look away with a sigh. I could blame it on the swimming, but it's this topic that makes my ribcage feel too tight, and my muscles tense all over. Just talking about that age-old incident brings with it a lifetime of baggage.

It's ridiculous, I know this. But that still doesn't make it easy to explain.

"It's just what?" he prompts.

If he'd sounded like a jerk about it, I could have laughed it off or changed the topic. But he sounds genuinely interested, like he really wants to know.

I stare straight ahead and watch the dark cloud approach. I've never put this into words before. Not to Celia or my mom...not even to myself. "I guess I get jealous."

I spit the words out like poison, and that's exactly how they taste. Bitter and toxic.

I feel his gaze on me and my cheeks burn. It's embarrassing to admit this aloud. But I can't keep swallowing this down either. I don't want to keep feeling this way. I don't want to keep *acting* this way. Those stories my friends told —yeah, most of them were from when we were little. But not all. And our style of fighting might have changed over the years, but that anger is still inside me and I hate it.

I don't know if talking is the answer, but it can't make things worse, right? And even if it doesn't do anything to end our rivalry, I think *I* need this. For me.

He's quiet beside me, but I can feel his tension, like he's afraid to move and wary of speaking.

I clear my throat. "Everyone else at Lakeview is just so..." I trail off because I don't have the words. I love my friends at Lakeview, and I don't begrudge them a thing. But that doesn't mean I don't have moments of resentment. "Everything seems to come so easily to everyone else. Money and grades and...everything." I turn to face him. "My parents enrolled me there when I was young and my dad was helping out with the bills, but ever since he left, my mom works crazy hours to pay that tuition and I bust my butt to maintain the partial scholarship..." Now that the words are coming out, they're coming fast and furious. Like they've just been waiting to tumble out of my mouth. "I always have to work a million times harder than anyone else. I can't let my grades slip, and I can't skip work if I feel like it, and I have to have extracurriculars for college applications, but I also have to work all year round, and I'm just..." A wave of unexpected emotions hit me, and I choke on the words. "I'm tired. I'm just so *tired*."

I stop the hailstorm of words when I see his face. His eyes are wide with surprise, and...something else. Something so sweet and tender it has me looking away quickly. I've been wearing a swimsuit all day, but right now I feel freakin' naked. I am vulnerable and exposed, and I have this horrible urge to cry, which is so not okay.

I swallow hard. "I guess even when I was eight years old I knew that things were different for you and the others. You guys were already in the lead and had every advantage."

I trail off, but he fills in the blanks. "So when I cheated to win, it was that much worse," he says.

I nod. "Yeah, I guess so. I mean, it sounds crazy now and I don't think I could have put any of that into words when I was eight, but—"

"I'm sorry." He reaches for me and tugs me into his arms before I know what's happening. It's an awkward side hug since we're sitting next to each other, but he squeezes me tight and says it again. "I'm really sorry."

I shrug as I pull away. "You were eight. I overreacted."

"Yeah, well, I should have said I'm sorry earlier."

A silence follows this admission, and I'm not sure how to feel. On one hand it's a relief. A weight's been lifted. But also...now there's a new tension here that I can't understand.

It's not *bad*. But I'm not necessarily comfortable either.

We see the rain coming before it hits, but then large raindrops are falling on us, and even though we're already wet, the rain is colder than the lake and I wrap my arms around my knees to stay warm.

Then a heavy arm is around my shoulders and I'm pressed against Ryan's side, and I am definitely warm.

I am so *very* warm.

I'm just starting to get used to this silence between us when Ryan breaks it suddenly. "I cheated because I liked you."

I stiffen under his arm. "What?"

He lets out this rueful laugh, and when I turn to face him, he's so unbearably handsome, it hurts. The rain is falling over his high cheekbones and down the sharp cut of his jaw. His dark hair is falling heavily over his forehead, and from the angle I can see droplets catch on his eyelashes.

"What did you just say?" I ask.

I can't look away from his mouth as his smile grows to something wicked, and I'm glad he keeps his gaze straight ahead so I don't get caught gaping at him. He makes a show of clearing his throat and readjusts his arm around me to keep me warm. "I, uh, I had a crush on you when we were kids."

I gasp. "You did not."

He nods, his brows arching. "I did."

"And so you cheated?" I'm sure he can hear my confusion, and he laughs.

"Yeah, well, I just wanted to get your attention." He glances over and there's so much mischievous laughter in his eyes, I feel like I'm getting a glimpse of the eight-year-old boy all over again. "I guess it worked, huh?"

My jaw is hanging open in sheer shock. "You...? You *liked* me?"

He shrugs and turns back to face the lake. I burrow in closer as the wind kicks up and makes me shiver.

"I was eight," he says. "You were cute. Of course I know now that pulling pigtails is lame, but eight year old me thought tugging on your leg and holding you back in the race would make you laugh."

"It didn't," I say. That obviously went without saying, but we both laugh softly at the understatement.

"Yeah, well, I know that *now*," he says.

I pull back slightly to get a better look at him. "Why are you telling me this?"

He shrugs, and I guess I know the answer. Because I'd apologized. Because we're trying to be more mature. Because it was ten years ago, and the past is in the past.

Because while he might have had a crush on me *then*, everything is different now.

The rain starts to come down even harder and we lean into each other on instinct. "I'm sorry I got us into this," I say as my teeth start to chatter.

"I'm sorry I let you win," he says.

"So you admit it!" I say as I jab his knee with a finger.

He laughs at me, and I tip my head down with a grin.

"While we're at it with the confessions..." He stops and takes a deep breath, and I can feel his chest expand next to mine. "You were right."

I blink over him, swiping rain out of my eyes as I study him. "Right about what?"

He gives me a quick sidelong glance. "I don't try unless I know I'm gonna win."

My lips part as I stare at him.

He goes back to staring straight ahead, and I see a muscle in his jaw tick. I know without having to be told that this is as hard for him as it was for me to admit to being jealous.

"I've been giving this a lot of thought ever since you said

it, and I realized that you're right. My parents expect a lot from me because of my brothers." He glances over and I nod.

That's the beauty of having known everyone in our school forever. I know all about his brothers. They're kind of legends at Lakeview, and Ryan has always been on track to follow in their footsteps.

Something that's only added to my hatred of the guy until right this second when I see it. Or I see a hint of it at least. I catch a glimpse of Ryan's reality, and maybe it's not all as perfect as it seems to be.

"And I guess, I never want to let them down. Or my brothers. Or everyone else at Lakeview who expects me to succeed at everything I do."

I nod slowly because...I can get that. The pressure to be the best. The expectation that you're a winner. I haven't moved an inch, but as I sit there and stare at Ryan's profile, my entire perspective flips. All at once I see this whole other side of him, and I swear that sudden shift has a physical effect. My belly dips and weaves like I'm on a roller coaster.

"And I..." He clears his throat. "I guess I'm not always the best at owning my mistakes either."

I'm shivering from the cold, but that's nothing compared to the way my heart starts to race in my chest. He sounds so genuine. So serious.

I'm not sure I've ever seen him so serious.

His gaze is fixed on the lake, but I know he's waiting on a response, and I have no idea what to say. So I end up echoing his words back to him to ease some of the seriousness of the moment. "How badly did it hurt to say that?"

He lets out a huff of laughter and shoots me a funny little lopsided smile. "A lot," he says. "It did *not* feel good."

I laugh when he repeats my words back to me. "Being the bigger person is really not all it's cracked up to be," I tease.

"It's highly overrated," he agrees. He looks at me as he says it, and I wait for him to turn back to face the lake. When he doesn't, when his gaze stays on me instead, roaming over me like he's trying to read me like a book, I forget all about the cold wind and the biting rain. The look in his eyes warms me all the way through even as it makes me nervous.

I'm not used to being this close to a guy. And while he's not making any moves, and his arm around me is just to keep me warm, I am still absurdly aware of his closeness. My belly is a pit of nerves at the newness of all these sensations, and my brain is racing with questions.

Would I be reacting this way to any guy?

Would I be burning up from the inside out if it were Ben sitting next to me with his arm around my shoulders?

I don't know. But...I don't think so.

"The storm cloud should pass soon," he says in this reassuring voice. It's only then I realize I've been shaking so hard he must be getting worried.

I nod. "I know."

One side of his mouth hitches up. "Any more confessions before it does?"

Before this moment in time is over, he means. Before we go back to our friends and our school and our life as we know it.

Any more confessions?

My gaze automatically drops to his lips. "Just one," I say.

His brows hitch up, but his eyes have gone dark. Darker

than the storm cloud overhead and so filled with desire I can't make my lungs work to take a much needed breath.

"What's that?" he asks.

"I lied when I said I'd been kissed before."

His gaze holds mine for so long, I start to question if I'd said the words aloud or if I'd blurted out that embarrassing truth in my head.

"That was your first kiss?" he finally asks. And when he does, I see his throat work, his Adam's apple bobbing as a muscle ticks in his jaw. He looks like he's struggling for control.

That makes two of us.

"That doesn't seem right," he says in a voice so low it's nearly drowned out by the wind. "Your first kiss shouldn't be part of a dare. You deserve better, don't you think?"

I clasp my hands together as I pull my knees in even tighter to my chest. All I can manage is a nod because his eyes are on my lips again.

"You know what I think we need?" His gaze lifts to meet mine when he talks.

"What?" I whisper.

He's already leaning in when he answers. "A do-over."

TWELVE

Ryan

I'M in the middle of a storm. Literally and metaphorically.

I'm barely aware of the rain pelting my back as I use a finger to tilt her chin up, and I don't feel the wind as I press my lips to hers. But it's the storm inside me that's raging out of control when she kisses me back. Tentatively at first, and then with more confidence.

Soon she's kissing me like she does everything in life— with authority. This fearless girl is exploring my mouth, tasting my lips, tilting her head as she figures out how we fit together.

Perfectly. That's how we fit.

Even at this awkward angle, sitting side by side and sheltering from a storm, it's perfect. When she sighs against my lips, I feel it everywhere. This ache. This need. This...affection.

I don't know how else to describe the tight swelling in my chest that's linked to the heat coursing through me. It's connected to it, but it's not the same. This isn't just physical desire, it's something more.

Her lips are so soft, I can barely stand it. I want to crush her to me even as I want to make sure I don't hurt her. I want to tug her closer, touch her everywhere. But I don't want to rush her, and I don't want to send her running. So I stay still. I let her lead. I follow her rhythm as she nips at my bottom lip and teasingly touches her tongue to mine, sending a jolt of electricity straight through to my spine.

When she shifts, lifting her hands and settling them on my chest, I groan at the sweet torture of it all. I could kiss her for hours. I could stay on this little island for the rest of my life and just kiss her.

But when she pulls back, I let her go. I watch in awe as she looks back at me with dazed eyes and draws in a deep, shaky breath, touching her fingers to her lips. I watch with that weird, aching sensation in my chest as her gaze focuses, as she comes back to reality. And I know.

I know that she felt it too. The perfection. The connection.

And that...

Well, that's freaking terrifying. At least, I have no idea what to make of this new thing between us. It feels fragile, and I don't trust myself to say a word.

So we just sit there. We huddle together, I wrap both arms around her in an attempt to keep her warm, and we stare at the lake as the last of rain hits before moving on.

In what feels like no time at all the storm cloud has passed, the lake is calm, and Mara and I are back to reality. A few more seconds of silence after the rain stops, and I'm starting to doubt any of that really happened.

I mean, it did. I know it did. But I don't know what it means.

Or if it means anything at all.

"Should we..." Mara glances over at me and her expression is uncharacteristically hesitant. "Should we go back?"

I nod. "Yeah." I stand up and help her to her feet. "Wanna race?"

She scoffs. "Yeah, right." She brushes the sand off her butt. "Kill myself trying to outswim you only to have you let me win? I don't think so."

I laugh because, just like that, we're back to normal.

Sort of.

I gesture toward the water before us with a flourish. "Ladies first."

"Oh sure, *now* he decides to be chivalrous," she mutters. But there's no real heat there, and by the time we make it back to shore and our friends—at a much more leisurely pace, I might add—all our friends know is that they saw us making out on the island.

So, in case there was any doubt about our new pseudo relationship, it's gone now.

We stick around for a little while, and then we help the others pack up as the sun starts to set and the air cools.

"You guys heading home or are you coming out with us?" Elijah asks. Heath, Leah, Ben, and a few others are hanging around.

I look to Mara. "What do you think?"

She seems surprised that I'm asking her what she wants to do. I know that I haven't been the most upstanding guy around Mara for...oh, ten years. But it's hard not to be slightly offended that she thinks so very little of me.

But then again, I was so surprised to see her laughing and smiling with her friends, and I'm guessing she'd be offended to know how shocked I was that she can relax and have fun.

It's possible we've both had a distorted view of each other after years of hating on one another.

She shifts closer to me, and while it might look to the others that she wants to be closer to her boyfriend, I know better. She's trying to be sneaky. With a nudge to my side and a hiss of a whisper I get that I'm supposed to step aside for a word in private. Even when we're a few steps away, and everyone else is happily talking amongst themselves, she casts the others a furtive stare.

It should be noted that Mara is not very good at being sneaky.

"So, did you want to hang out with the others or head home?" I ask.

"I think you need to live up to your end of our bargain." She arches her brows meaningfully, and for a full second all I can do is stand there and stare.

Man, she is so pretty. She was hot the other night with her sexy hair and makeup and the leather skirt, but I've never been more attracted to anyone than I am right now as I take her in in all her makeupless glory. As the sun set, she'd thrown on an oversized sweatshirt and some track pants. Her hair is more tousled and unruly than ever, and stray locks form a sort of halo around her face. She's got this healthy glow from a summer spent lifeguarding, and without makeup she looks as innocent as she is.

My lungs refuse to work as I struggle to draw in a normal breath. She tilts her head to the side with a quizzical little frown, and I realize I have yet to respond to what she'd said.

Not only that, our friends are waiting on us before they take off for wherever they're going.

"Sorry, what did you say?" I ask.

Mara smiles and nudges my side with her elbow. "I *said,*

you've got to keep up your end of the deal." She widens her eyes meaningfully again, waiting for me to catch on.

When I do it feels like a punch in the gut.

My gaze darts from her to Ben.

Ben. The guy she likes. Is that what this is about? But before I can ask, she loses patience and snags me by my bicep. She's dragging me toward my car as she tells the others. "Sorry, guys, but I need Ryan tonight."

This gets a whole lot of wolf whistles and catcalls from my friends, but she rolls her eyes and ignores them.

I stare at her in surprise. "Where are we going?"

Her grin is outright wicked. "To a strip club."

My brain goes blank. I'm pretty sure I've lost my mind. And when it starts working again, all I can think of are the terms of our deal. I'm supposed to get her Ben at the end of all this. That was the deal.

The thought weighs on me, dragging at my gut and making my stomach turn.

Crap. I don't want to hand her Ben on a platter.

I don't want to see her with Ben at all.

I'm so focused on that, I barely even comprehend what she'd said until we're at my car and I'm opening her car door. "Wait. Why am I taking you to a strip club?"

Her smile is so sweet and wholesome I can't believe we're talking about strippers. "The scavenger hunt?" She arches her brows.

Right. I nod. Of course. The scavenger hunt.

The flood of relief that we're not talking about her winning over Ben makes me slump against her car door for a second after I close it.

"If you're going to help me, I'm gonna need you to get the application for the strip club," she informs me when I slide into the driver's seat.

"For what?"

She shrugs. "A male stripper, I guess?"

I turn to stare. "You're evil."

She gives me a little bop on the nose. "Then I guess you made a deal with the devil."

I choke on a laugh because this...?

This is definitely not a side of Mara I've ever seen. And I like it.

I like it a lot.

I turn on the car and start to back out of the parking lot. "So the strip club thing, does it really have to be tonight?"

I glance over and see her pursing her lips. "Why? Did you want to go out with your friends?"

"No," I say quickly. And I mean it. I love my friends, but I've been loving having alone time with Mara more. "But you do know the scavenger hunt won't end for a while yet, right? It *can't* end."

She nods. "I know. Some of the items on the list can't be checked off until after the school year starts." She winces. "Like that one about interrupting a pep rally?"

She looks so terrified, I can't help but laugh. "Exactly. So why do we need to start tonight?"

"Because there's no time like the present," she says. And there she is. Miss Perfect. My little straight-A over-achiever.

But for the first time in our lives, this part of her makes me grin. Maybe it's because now I know there's more to her than this. She's responsible and competitive and smart and maybe a little holier than thou.

But she's also loyal, empathetic, funny...and she can even be fun when she feels like it.

And on top of that—she has no problem calling me out. She's honest and straightforward, and never avoids conversations or experiences just because they're difficult or she might fail.

I admire the girl, plain and simple.

And honestly? I want her to admire me. Lame as it might sound, I want to impress her. I want to make her smile.

And I want to prove to her that I'm not the guy she'd thought I was. Not entirely at least.

I drive us to the strip club, and once we're there I turn to her with arched brows. "You don't think I'll go through with this, do you?"

She presses her lips together like she's trying not to laugh as she lifts one shoulder in a shrug. "I want to see you prove me wrong."

"Done." I've already reached for the door handle as I speak, and I see her eyes widen in surprise. I lean forward and steal a kiss which only seems to stun her further because she's outright gaping at me when I climb out.

But even better is the look on her face when I return. A success, thank you very much. I hand over the application with a flourish. "Never underestimate a Hunter," I say with a smirk I know she hates.

But instead of answering with her usual snarl, her head falls back with a laugh. She holds the application up to read it. "Never," she says. And then she adds, "Never again."

"Where to next?" I ask. "Please tell me you don't want me to twerk on a statue tonight." I give her a grimace. "I'm kinda beat."

She nods and covers a yawn. "Me too. And sadly enough, I have to be at school in the morning."

"School?" I arch my brows in question.

She nods. I don't miss the way she ducks her head, hiding her face a bit.

I shift uneasily. "Is this a Ben thing?"

"Sort of. He'll be there for yearbook stuff, and we're supposed to meet and talk about student council plans."

I resist the urge to mock this. Not because I think it's lame that she's so into student council and our school. It's kind of...cute, or whatever. But there's a swell of possessiveness that makes it hard to breathe.

And if I'm trying hard to face the truth these days, I can admit that maybe it's jealousy.

Maybe I'm freakin' jealous as hell of Ben the Bore. I'm jealous that Mara honestly likes him. She respects and admires him, and she actually wants to spend time with him.

Ben would never have to trap her into playing the part of his girlfriend.

"But also," she says in this tight little voice. "I have to go fill out my scholarship paperwork and figure out how we can swing the rest of the tuition bill."

The words sit heavily between us and that ache in my chest? It feels like a freakin' spear because I *know*. I know exactly how hard that is for her to say. To me, at least. This girl has more pride than anyone I've ever met, and she hates letting anyone see her vulnerabilities.

Especially me.

I'm beyond touched. I'm grateful that she trusts me. Or, she's starting to, at least. But I have no idea how I'm supposed to respond.

"You need a ride?" I finally say.

She glances over at me in surprise, and I know what she's thinking. I don't have to drive her to school. It's not like anyone would know. But I also know she doesn't have a car.

And yeah, okay. I can admit the truth. Maybe I want to see her again.

Maybe I don't want to wait until the next gathering of friends to have more time alone with her. Maybe I'm starting to realize just how little time I have left until Leah leaves and this agreement with Mara ends.

She's silent for a little too long, and her expression is hard to read when I look over.

This is another test. I don't mean for it to be, but it is. She might be okay with accepting rides and help from her friends, but from me?

She wets her lips and turns to face forward. "That would be great." She glances over with a shy smile that makes my heart feel wrung out like a dish rag. "Thanks."

THIRTEEN

Mara

MY MOM'S watching me race around the apartment to get ready, her feet kicked up on the edge of the loveseat and a mug of coffee dangling from her hand. "Tell me again why you're going to school when you don't have to?"

I ignore the teasing because she knows perfectly well that I have student council business to attend to and then a late shift at the country club. My days there are numbered and I've been trying to work every available shift I can until school gets underway and the pool shuts down entirely.

"And then maybe you can explain to me where you came from." My mom lifts her head to take a sip of coffee and falls back against the cushions again. "Because you certainly didn't come from me."

I turn to face her. "How do I look?"

She eyes the earrings I put in—a rarity for me—plus my hair, which I actually blow dried into a semi-straight sheet.

One hit of humidity when I walk out the door and it'll be in vain, but I give myself an A for effort.

My mom does too, judging by the way her brows arch like she's impressed by what she sees. "Love the hair, ditch the cardigan."

I purse my lips as I take in my outfit. "But it's air-conditioned in the high school."

She waves a hand toward her bedroom. "Then borrow my pink open-knit sweater to wear over the sundress."

"Yeah?" But I don't bother waiting for reassurance. My mom knows way more about style than I do, which is probably just a little bit pathetic considering I'm the younger one here. A few seconds later I come out sporting her top and she's all smiles. "Now it's perfect."

I grin, heading toward the front door.

"Not so fast." My mom's sitting upright, and I know her expression well.

I'm already edging toward the door when the questions begin. "Does this have something to do with the boy you like?"

"Mom—"

"What's his name? How'd you meet? What's he into? Is he in your class?"

I open my mouth and then shut it. Shock renders me speechless. What's his name?

My first thought was Ryan. Which is wrong. But with each question, the answers kept popping into my head and they were all about Ryan.

The wrong guy.

"Um..."

My mom purses her lips and gives me the ultimate Mom look—and I'm pretty sure that in this moment, at least, she can read my mind. Or at the very least, she knows

I'm freaked. I can't say for sure if she knows that the boy I like is Ben-from-student-council or that I'd accidentally kissed Ryan-the-enemy instead, but I swear she knows something.

"Honey, is there something you want to tell me?" she asks.

I shrug. "It's just... It's confusing, that's all." *What with the fake boyfriend and the real kiss and the old crush and all.*

"Oh yes," she says with a sigh as she sinks back into the couch. "It always is."

I try not to wince, but I think I fail. I know what my mom's thinking about. She's thinking about my dad. Her first love and the guy who gave her me. Everything changed for her when she fell for my dad—and not necessarily in a good way. You know, except for me.

But somehow, she still wants me to have a first love. She's just dying for me to have a real high school boyfriend. Even now, I can see her eyes getting all soft with memories, and any second now she's going to start in on how you only live once and how I should seize the day and, if I'm not quick enough in my escape, there might be some quoting of *Dead Poets Society* going on.

"Want to tell me about him?" she asks.

Once again, I open my mouth and close it without speaking. Yet again, my first instinct had been to talk about Ryan. About the confusing mix of emotions I've been stewing in ever since we'd talked. And then kissed. And then had a surprisingly nice ride home together after swinging by a strip club.

But she's not asking about my fake beau, she's asking about my *crush*.

Which is Ben.

It would just be really great if I could remember that.

Especially since I'm on my way to see him now. I mean, that's why I made the effort with my appearance, right?

Right?

"You okay? Because you're gonna get wrinkles if you keep frowning like that," my mom helpfully points out.

I sigh. "I'm fine, it's just..." *I don't know if I made an effort to look nice for my crush or my fake boyfriend. On a scale of one to ten, how messed up is that?*

Now my mom's the one in danger of getting wrinkles because her brows are knitted in concern. "Sweetie? Is there something wrong?"

"No." It comes out on autopilot because much as my mom loves me and is there for me, I don't like to add to her worries. She has enough on her plate as it is. And besides, this isn't a real dilemma, right? Because as far as Ryan is concerned, we have a set end date, and once Leah leaves, he and I will go our separate ways.

I'll hopefully be off to a nice future with Ben, and he'll be off to a future with...someone else. I can't picture who. It could be anyone. But the more I try to envision him with some other girl, the more my stomach clenches in discomfort.

But the point is, we'd both move on and all confusion would end. And maybe we'd even part as friends.

Just like that my mind decides to replay that kiss on the island. My breath leaves me in a whoosh, and my legs forget they're made of solid muscle and bone. There'd been nothing friendly about that kiss.

Is it possible to think of him as a friend after a kiss like that?

I guess I'll find out soon enough.

A knock on the door gives me a start, and I turn to stare at it in horror. It's Ryan. He's supposed to pick me up, but I hadn't expected him to come to my door. Who walks up to a third-floor apartment on the far end of the complex when he can just text that he's there?

As I walk to answer it, I check my phone to see if I'd missed a text. I shove it back in my pocket because nope—I hadn't missed anything.

Yet, sure enough, there he is. All six-feet of cocky arrogance called Ryan. "Hey," he says. His gaze rakes over me instantly, and I feel it all the way to my core. "You look nice."

"Thanks." I'm about to shove him right back out the door, but my mom has other plans.

"Who's here?" But she sees him. From where she's sitting she can see him perfectly fine. "Oh, Ryan! Is that you?"

I roll my eyes as I open the door wider. *Is that you?* Is that what she went with?

Of course it's him. She's seen him no less than a million times over the years, and she knows very well who he is. But it gets worse as she starts to compliment him on how much he's grown, how much he's filled out. I cringe as I listen because my mom's not *trying* to sound like a cougar...but I'm pretty sure she sounds like a cougar.

Or maybe I'm just paranoid.

She flashes me a funny little grin as she heads toward the kitchen with an offer to feed him.

How she's going to feed him in the three seconds we have before we need to be out the door, I don't know.

But her wicked grin is making me suspect that she's trying to embarrass me. I let out a little sigh and force myself to relax.

My mom will only try harder if I get all uptight about it. Sometime when I was a toddler, my mom apparently decided that it's her mission in life to make sure I don't take life too seriously.

For the most part, she's failed. And then I got old enough that she stopped trying to make me lighten up all the time. She's even started to accept that I'm highly competitive and won't quit until I earn a scholarship to a good school.

But there are still moments like this one when she really brings her A-game.

"Thanks, Mrs.—"

"Monique, please," my mom says. Which is her way of nicely avoiding that awkward moment when she has to explain that she's no longer married to my dad, hadn't taken his name during that uber brief period when they *had* been married, and wouldn't marry him again if he was the last man on earth.

Not that it's awkward for *her*. Just me. She seems to relish this conversation when it comes up—with the well meaning grocery store clerk, the Lakeview High principal, the librarian, or that one time with the police officer who pulled her over for speeding. Bet he hadn't expected to get an earful about her marital status, but them's the breaks when you try to give Monique Hayes a ticket.

"Um, thanks, *Monique*," Ryan says. "But I should get Mara here to school before she gives herself an ulcer at the thought of being late."

My mom throws her head back with a laugh like this is the most hilarious thing she's ever heard. Ryan shoots me a smirk. It's the same smirk that's always driven me insane, but today it doesn't make me angry.

It makes me want to laugh like my mom's laughing.

"It's funny because it's true," my mom says through her laughter.

I settle for a smile and an eye roll. "You two are hilarious," I say.

Ryan turns to me. "Ready to head out?"

I nod, ignoring my mom's over-the-top mouthing and pointing behind his back. *Is this him? Is he the one?*

I give my head a quick shake as I reach for his arm and drag him out in the hallway. I'm not sure if he saw that little exchange or not.

Until we reach the stairwell, that is.

"So, I'm not *the one*, huh?" His voice is mild, his gaze teasing, and I...I forget how to function like a human being.

"I didn't—I wasn't—" I stumble over words and then my own two feet. I catch myself on the handrail before I can tumble down the steps.

"Whoa." He catches my elbow to help steady me. "I was just kidding."

"I know." I sound too defensive. "I mean, I *know*."

Nope. That wasn't any better.

He lets it slide as we head down the last flight. But when we burst out into the warm morning sun, he turns to me with a lopsided smile that makes my belly flip. "So, I take it you didn't tell your mom about me?"

I shrug. "What's there to tell?"

"Right," he says. I can't read his tone, and when I glance over, the sun is glaring behind him so I can't read his face either.

"Why?" I say. "Did you tell your parents about me?"

He gives a short laugh. "Of course not."

We reach his car, and I'm still trying to decide if I should be insulted by that. "Of course not," I finally say. "It's not going to last long enough that they need to know."

He's silent, but he reaches for my door handle and opens the car door for me like he's some suave gentleman from another era. It throws me for a second, and for the second time since he's arrived, I'm fumbling over words. "I mean, we're going to be ending this soon, right? As soon as Leah leaves, right? That's the deal, so what's the point?"

"I knew what you meant," he says. He closes the car door behind me, and I feel like I just gave the wrong answer on a test.

But that's stupid because neither of us told our parents about this. So, why on earth do I feel guilty?

I turn to face him and I have every intention of asking him why he's acting weird, but then he's *not* acting weird. At all. His smile is relaxed as he turns the key in the ignition, and I start to wonder about my own sanity. Maybe I'm the only one acting weird here.

"So what was your mom freaking out about back there?" he asks. "Who'd she think I was?" His hands shift on the wheel. "Ben?"

"Um, sort of," I say slowly.

He arches a brow and glances over me like he's waiting for an explanation.

"Celia kind of told her that I like someone. But my mom doesn't know who."

"Ah," he says. And he's back to being unreadable. "And now she's dying to find out who."

"Yeah." I shrug. "She'll find out eventually."

"Because you tell her everything?" he asks. There's something in his voice that tugs at my chest and I don't know why.

"Not *everything*," I say. But after a beat, I add, "But what I don't tell her, Celia does."

He bursts out in a laugh at that. "Celia spills your secrets to your mom?"

I nod, a laugh bubbling up in response to his laughter.

"Yeah. You know, it doesn't feel that weird to me because I'm used to it. But admitting it out loud is making me wonder if maybe my relationship with my mom is a little weird."

"She's nice," Ryan says. I love the little smile that hovers over his lips. A remnant of his laughter. "She's got so much personality. She's..." His jaw works like he's mulling over his words. "She's fearless." He glances over. "Like you."

"Me?" I widen my eyes in shock when I realize he's not kidding. "I'm definitely not fearless. Actually, my mom would laugh her butt off if she heard you say that I am."

"Why's that?"

I don't live far from school, and he's pulling off onto our street all too soon.

"Because she's always trying to get me to lighten up. To let loose. To worry less and experience more..." I trail off with a shrug. "It's not that I don't want to experience things. I do. It's just..."

"You can't let anything drop either," he says. "You're juggling a lot, and you can't afford to fail."

I stare at him in silence for a long second. "Yeah. That's it exactly."

"I get it," he says. Then he turns to me with that smirk I know so well. "I mean, I'm not in the same boat, but I get it."

Because he also feels like he can't fail. Not because he'll lose a scholarship or leave his parents hanging when he can't help with the bills, but because he doesn't want to let anyone down.

So no, it's not the same.

But yes, he totally gets it.

As if to prove his point, he adds, "Is that why you're so intent on taking part in the scavenger hunt?"

I nod. "Yeah. It's not about winning—"

"Excuse me?" He pulls up in front of the curb and stops, turning to me with wide eyes as he does. "It's *not* about winning? Who are you, and what have you done to Mara?"

I start to laugh, and he joins me. "Okay, fine. It's partially about winning—"

"Uh huh."

"But it's also about doing...stuff."

My breath catches as my gaze meets his, and his lips curve up at the corners. "Stuff, huh?"

"Stuff," I repeat like a moron. I feel like an idiot. I can barely form words when he's looking at me like this. No taunting. Maybe a little teasing. But no judgement. Just...affection.

That's the lamest word I can think of, but it's the only one that fits. His gorgeous blue eyes are softened with it, and his smile has none of its caustic edge.

He leans in slightly, and I hold my breath. My gaze drops to his lips because...he's going to kiss me. And I want him to.

"Don't look now," he says softly. "But *the one* is right behind you."

"The...what?" I can't speak. I can barely function. I blink as I realize two things at once.

Ryan is not going to kiss me.

And Ben is standing right outside my car door.

FOURTEEN

Ryan

I'VE NEVER ONCE in my life wished to have more football practices. I like the game because I'm good at it, but it's not my passion or anything. But today I'm actually annoyed that we don't have practice because I have nothing better to do than stand around and wait for Mara to get done flirting with *the one.*

And yes, I saw her mother say that. I actually heard it too because she was standing right next to me, and the words slipped out on a breath. *Is he the one?*

Met with a big old shake of Mara's head.

No. Of course not. She might as well have spit on the ground in disgust.

Okay fine, maybe I'm overreacting. No, I'm definitely overreacting. But I can't help it. I'm not exactly feeling like my most rational self right now, and I absolutely blame the kiss. The first kiss, the second kiss—the kiss that almost happened in the car just now.

She would have kissed me back. I saw the way her eyelids got all heavy, her gaze all dark and seductive. She wanted to kiss me too.

Until she realized Ben was waiting for her, and then she jerked away from me like she'd been electrocuted and reached for the door handle.

I could have made a joke about how she needed to play it cool. She *was* trying to make the guy jealous, after all.

But I hadn't said a word.

Nope. I'd just sat there and watched her scramble out of the car. I heard her cheerful greeting to Ben right before she slammed the door shut behind her and walked away.

So fine. Good.

I throw a basketball and hit the backboard. It bounces off with a loud thud, and I chase after it. I don't know how long she's gonna be. I do know she has work this afternoon. I figure she'll need a ride.

So here I am. Waiting around like an idiot for a girl who's not even my real girlfriend.

Something is very wrong with this picture.

"Ryan! Hey!"

I tense automatically at the sound of Leah's voice, and it takes a full second for me to remember that I have nothing to be afraid of these run-ins anymore. "Leah, hey," I say.

"You here for football?" she asks.

I nod toward the school. "Mara's got some student council stuff."

"Awww," she says in a sing-song tone that makes me cringe. Also, I have no idea why this is worthy of an *awww*.

"Are you guys going to the bonfire this weekend?" she asks.

"Of course. Wouldn't miss it." I aim and throw. "Will you be there? You'll still be in town, right?"

She doesn't answer instantly. I catch the bouncing ball and tuck it under my arm as I turn to face her. I have this flicker of panic at Leah's hesitation.

But her smile is bright when she finally answers. "Yeah, I'll be there."

I let out a breath. Leah will be there. Which means Mara will be there with me. The fact that I can now breathe easily is alarming, to say the least. A few days ago, Mara was my worst nightmare. The bane of my existence. So why am I so anxious to keep her at my side?

I glance over at the school with a frown. And why do I hate that she's in there alone with Ben?

I think I know the answer. I'm not that much of an idiot. But I don't want to think about it. Not right now. Not when Mara is with Ben, and when she's so hellbent on ending up with him the moment she's free to break up with me.

There's a tension in my neck and shoulders, and it's spreading to my limbs. I'm not big on feelings—talking about them or even *feeling* them. I definitely don't enjoy acknowledging them. But there's no denying that I'm feeling something for Mara. She's *making* me feel things. She's making me talk about feelings, and think about feelings, and she's bringing all kinds of emotions I'd never even looked at before out of the dark and into the light, and—

And I'm losing it.

I give my head a shake as Leah continues her small talk. Luckily, she doesn't seem to expect much by the way of answers because I need to get my head on straight before Mara comes back out here.

I was reacting like a jealous boyfriend back at Mara's house and in the car, but that's not okay. I'm not allowed to be a jealous boyfriend if I'm not even her real boyfriend.

And if I were her real boyfriend?

I still. I tense. I watch Leah's mouth move as my brain goes into a death spiral.

Is that what I want?

My whole body goes numb for a second, and I'm standing there like a statue as my brain slowly and haltingly goes back to work. Do I really want to make Mara Loman my girlfriend? For real?

I think...I think maybe I do.

But what if she doesn't want me? The thought is terrifying, there's no other word for it.

But I've got time to figure this out. To make her see that this isn't all fake between us. At least, the chemistry is very, very real, and maybe there could even be more there, if we just give it some time.

Time. That's all I need. Then I can sort out what I want and make Mara see that she wants it too.

"Do you want to know a secret?" Leah asks, cutting into my thoughts and making me blink as I realize I've been standing there silent for way too long. Leah's shifting from foot to foot in front of me. Do I want to know her secret?

I don't think I could stop her from spilling her secret if I tried.

"Sure," I say.

She leans forward and lowers her voice to a whisper. "I'm not leaving." She gives me this crazy big grin as I try to make sense of what she's saying.

"What? What do you mean?" I ask. "Like, you're not leaving right away or—"

"No. Like, I'm going to be going to school with you guys starting next week." Her statement ends on a high squeak of excitement.

I stare until her smile starts to fade. Only then do I

realize I've said nothing. "Wow," I say, hoping sheer volume makes me sound elated by this news. "I mean, just...*wow*."

It seems to work because her smile is back and it's beaming. "I know, right?"

"Yeah, I mean..." I run a hand through my hair as my heart rate ticks up. "How did I not know about this?"

She claps her hands together looking totally delighted by herself. "That's why it's a secret. No one knows. Not yet. I'd been waiting to make sure it was a done deal before I spread the word."

"Wow," I say again. I don't know why.

"Yeah, I'll tell everyone soon, but there's just been so much to figure out, you know? So many logistics, and we had to get my dad on board and then make sure all of my classes would transfer and..."

She's still talking but the words have stopped making sense. I'm too busy trying to figure out what this means to me.

If Leah's not leaving, then we don't have an end date.

But if Leah's here forever then...we can't keep up this pretense until the end of the year.

Unless it's not a pretense.

I am painfully aware of the fact that even now Mara might be having the time of her life inside with Ben. Which is good.

Good for her.

The moment I think it, my hands clench and my jaw goes tight. Nope. That thought's not gonna fly. I'm not as selfish as Mara's always made me out to be but I'm not some martyr either. I don't know where this thing with her is heading, but I want to find out.

And I sure as hell don't want to see her get together with Ben before I have the chance.

"Mum's the word for now though, 'kay?" Leah asks.

My shoulders start to loosen as I see my loophole—

"But of course you can tell Mara." She rolls her eyes. "Obviously. I wouldn't want to make you keep a secret from your girlfriend."

That tension is back. I can tell Mara. But will I?

I'll have to, right?

Eventually, at least.

Time is running out no matter how I look at it.

My mouth goes weirdly dry, and luckily Leah fills the silence because I'm not even sure I'm capable of speech right now.

"Here she comes now," Leah says.

My head snaps up to follow her gaze to the side entrance of the school where Mara is walking out the door. Her head is bent down and she's laughing. Ben's at her side and he's smiling too. Just a couple of happy kids.

How sweet.

I don't realize what my face is doing until Mara's head comes up and she spots me—and her laughter stops short. Her smile falls at the sight of me. Or maybe at the scowl I'm wearing.

Yup. A quick assessment of the facial features assures me that I am indeed glaring at the two of them. Ben's footsteps falter, and he slows his pace so he's a half step behind Mara when they approach.

Mara's smile is back as she takes in me, Leah, and the basketball.

"Hey," she says, sounding breathless. "You waited."

"Yeah, I thought you might need a ride to work."

She stares at me like she's never seen me before, and I feel like the world's largest dork.

"Oh, uh..." She glances over at Ben, who gives her a

little wince that seems to say *well, this is awkward.* "Ben offered to give me a ride." Her eyes widen as they meet mine, and I see a flicker of guilt there. Like she actually cheated on me.

Or maybe she just feels bad for wasting my time.

"I didn't know you were going to wait," she adds quietly.

"It's fine if you want to go with Ryan," Ben says. "I was going to head to the lake anyway, and that's the other direction."

"I was going to go to the lake too," Leah says, like it's the most amazing coincidence of all time. It really isn't considering it's where most of our classmates hang out when the weather is nice and they have nothing else to do.

"You need a ride?" Ben asks.

Leah beams. "I'd love that." Said with all the enthusiasm of someone offered a first-class trip to Italy and not a ride to the other side of town.

Mara and I watch them go off together, Leah chatting a mile a minute, before we walk back toward my car.

"Thanks for staying," she says. Her tone is hesitant, which I'm not used to. I'm not sure what to make of it.

"Not a big deal," I say. "I had nothing else to do."

"Oh. Right." She stares straight ahead as I drive us out of the parking lot and head toward the club. "Are you gonna hang out for a while? I think Bianca's working the front desk, and Freddy is at the bar. He'd love some company, and I—"

She cuts herself off, and I glance over. "You what?"

She doesn't immediately respond, and I hate how tense I am. I hate how much I'm hanging on her words.

I hate that seeing her with Ben so thoroughly messed with my head.

But mainly, I hate that Leah just gave me a reason to end this thing between us. And I don't want to. But the moment I tell Mara, she's going to insist on breaking up.

I was supposed to have days left to figure this out, not hours.

I'm not ready to let her go, not until I figure out how I feel. Not until I make her feel it too.

We sit in silence until I reach the country club parking lot. The sight of a familiar SUV has me muttering a curse under my breath.

"What's wrong?" Mara asks.

"My parents are here. They probably met friends for lunch."

"Oh." Her hands are fidgeting with her bag in her lap. She's been doing that since we got in the car, and it's not like her. She seems nervous, and I hate that because it puts me on edge. Some weird new paranoid section of my brain is wondering why she's so uncomfortable.

Is it guilt? Did she flirt with Ben when they were working together? Did she kiss him? Did she find out about Leah staying somehow?

"So, do you wanna park or..." She's eyeing me oddly, and I realize I've stopped the car in the middle of the parking lot and there's a car behind me waiting to move forward.

I quickly pull into a spot.

"I guess I'll go in and say hi," I say. "Hang out with you and the others on duty. You know...if you want."

I wish I could call the words back on the sheer basis of how lame they sound. *If you want?* Crap. Who am I right now and where is my confidence? Where's my notorious swagger?

Mara looks as confused as I feel as she glances at the

club and then back to me. "Do you, um...do *you* want to?" She wets her lips and I nearly groan aloud because I want to kiss her. I want to kiss her so much it's all I can focus on.

But she's acting hesitant or nervous or something and that makes me nervous.

Which is weird.

I don't do nervous.

But I also don't do...this. Fake relationships, obviously. But also...this. Whatever this is where we talk about real crap and spill our feelings, or whatever.

I don't do relationships, I guess. Fake or otherwise. So I don't know what she's thinking or what I'm supposed to be doing.

"If you're worried about them seeing us together," she says, "I can just go first and—"

"What?" I interrupt. "Why would you do that?"

Her cheeks are turning pink. "I know you don't want your parents to know about me so—"

"Mara, I'm not embarrassed to have you as my girlfriend, if that's what you're thinking." The words blurt out of me because I'm so horrified at the suggestion.

"I wasn't thinking that," she mutters. Her cheeks pinken even more and I know that she's lying.

That's exactly what she was thinking. It was written all over her face. And that's just infuriating for some reason I can't explain.

Both the fact that she thinks anyone would be embarrassed to be with her like that and that I'm so shallow that I'd be worried about what my parents think of my girlfriend.

"Look at me, Mara," I say.

She turns, and when our gazes clash, I feel it. "If you were really my girl, I'd be proud as hell to introduce you to my parents."

Her eyes widen, but she doesn't say anything.

"And they'd love you," I add.

Her brows draw together in disbelief. "Really?"

"Really." I tap my hands on the steering wheel.

Call me an insensitive, self-absorbed jerk, but it's only now that I'm really starting to understand just how much being the poor kid at a school full of wealthy brats has affected her. It explains so much, really. Her pride and her anger, her determination and her insecurities.

"If you say so," she says quietly as she drops her gaze back down to the bag in her lap.

She doesn't believe me. I don't know how I know it, but I know.

It's like I've found the cipher that makes sense of Mara. But it's not a cipher, obviously. And she's not some cryptic riddle. She's human and she's vulnerable, even though she goes to great lengths to hide it.

My heart is a freakin' aching mess in my chest as all this clicks into place. I've seen this new side of her because she's let me in. She's been open and honest with me, and it's impossible not to give the same in return.

"It's the fact that they'll love you," I say suddenly, before I can stop myself. "That's why I don't want them to know."

"Oh." Her expression says this makes no sense to her.

I let out a sharp exhale. "They'll love you, and when this is over, they'll be disappointed."

I'll be disappointed.

I suck in air as I realize it's the truth—and it's an epic understatement. I won't just be disappointed, I'll be crushed.

"Really?" she says. For a second, I wonder if she's read my mind.

"Really."

"So you don't want them to know about us because it's not going to last," she says.

She says it so matter of factly it feels like a kick in the gut. "Exactly."

"Okay." She nods. "I get that, I guess."

I start to let out a relieved exhale when she adds, "I meant to ask, what were you and Leah talking about?"

I stare at her. "What?"

Her lips are curving up in that delicious smile that I used to hate and now kinda love. The one that says she thinks I'm an idiot. "You and Leah?" she says. "Did she say anything about us?"

"No. No we were just talking about..." I trail off because —this is it. This is when I could tell her what Leah said. This is when I could tell her...and then she would insist that we end this fake relationship because it's not like it can go on forever, right?

Right?

She waves a hand in my face. "Hello? Earth to Ryan."

I laugh. Man, she is so pretty when she's smiling at me like that. She's so pretty, and so brave, and so sweet...

And she's mine.

For right now, at least, she's mine.

"We were talking about the bonfire," I finish. "She wanted to make sure we were going."

"You said yes, right?" she asks, her eyes all eager with excitement. "We have to go. It's a senior year ritual."

I laugh. "Of course we're going." On impulse I grab her hand and bring it to my lips. "We're going together."

FIFTEEN

Mara

WE'RE GOING TOGETHER.

I can't stop hearing Ryan's voice in my head, and it's annoying. Celia tugs on my hair and I yelp, but she goes right back to talking to Addie like my scalp and its pain aren't worthy of her time.

Meanwhile, I continue to meet my gaze in the reflection of the mirror over Celia's vanity. Me, myself, and I are having something of a showdown as I try to rid my brain of thoughts of Ryan.

We're going together.

I swear my hand is still tingling from where he kissed it.

And also...who kisses hands? At what point had Ryan Hunter done a body swap with Cary Grant? If you'd told me a week ago that Ryan Hunter was secretly a chivalrous gentleman beneath that arrogant smirking oversized ego of his I would have laughed myself sick.

We're going together.

I shake my head to make the loop of his voice stop.

It's not like he meant anything by it. He was being literal. It was a pragmatic statement about the logistics of our plan. That was all.

We're going together.

I frown at my reflection. So why can't I stop replaying it? There was something in his voice or the way he was looking at me.

Something that I can't shake. Something that I don't understand.

"Okay, I'm just gonna say it," Celia says as she steps back to admire her handiwork. "I have outdone myself."

I give a little snort of laughter, but Addie and Noelle are already fussing over how great I look. I turn my head this way and that as I take in her handiwork. "You really are a miracle worker, Celia."

She grins, and when she does, she resembles a doll...in the least creepy way possible. She's all pale skin, delicate features, and pink lips and cheeks. She leans over and adds one last bobby pin to secure the braids she's woven into a crown around my head. "Maybe this way you'll get through tonight's party without a wind-whipped disaster on your hands," she says.

Addie claps her hands together. "I can't wait to see Ryan's reaction. You look hot."

Hot? I'm not so sure about that. I look down at my very ordinary jeans and the long-sleeved top I'd borrowed from my mom. It's not exactly formalwear, but I do feel good tonight. In the mirror, there's no denying the pink in my cheeks or the way my eyes are lit up with excitement.

Excitement and nerves.

Or maybe anticipation?

I don't really know what this feeling is, but it's like

bubbles in my veins. I don't want to sit still, but I don't know what to do with myself either. It's not like I can leave. Ryan's coming here to pick me up. Most of our friends are meeting up here first since Celia's got a huge house and parents who don't care who hangs out, or even who crashes.

"Ryan's going to love this look," Noelle says as she comes over to study me with a critical eye.

I wince. "You guys do remember that I'm not really *with* Ryan, right?"

Yeah, that's right. My friends know. Of course they do. I'm a terrible liar, and they know me too well to believe I'd actually gone and fallen for my enemy. Although, the word enemy doesn't really fit him anymore. So what does that make him? A friend?

I shift uncomfortably in my seat as my brain helpfully calls up a vivid reminder of that kiss on the island.

Nope. *Friend* doesn't fit him either.

"You're *kind of* with Ryan," Addie says. "I mean, you're with him temporarily, right? That still counts."

I open my mouth and shut it. Honestly, I feel like Addie really wants me to be with him. She's a romantic like that, and seeing us together the other day had her convinced that there's something real between us.

I go to remind her that there isn't, but the words just won't come out.

We'll go together.

Yes, that is the super helpful refrain I hear in my brain instead.

"Mara's right," Noelle says. "Who cares what Ryan thinks? What matters is what Ben thinks. Right?"

I open my mouth, and for a second time, I close it without saying a word. When I realize they're all still watching me, I smile. "Actually, the only thing that matters is what I think." I reach out and squeeze Celia's hand. "And I love it. Thank you."

She's still grinning as she heads over to her closet to figure out what she's wearing. "How cold do we think it'll get?" she asks. "Too cold for this?"

She holds up a super skimpy dress that makes me wince at the thought of how cold she'd be wearing that by the lake, which is notoriously windy at night. "Definitely too cold for that."

"August in Miami would be too cold for that," Addie adds with a laugh.

"Seriously," Noelle says, though there's a note of approval in her voice. "Where's sexy Celia coming from?" She goes over and tugs on Celia's braid. "I'm used to preppy Celia and cute-as-a-button Celia, but slutty Celia?" She reaches for the dress to take a closer look.

We're all laughing as Celia pulls it out of reach. "It's not slutty."

"Fine," Noelle agrees easily. "But it is sexy."

"I like it," Addie says.

"Me too," I add. "But it's definitely not your normal look. Especially not for a bonfire by the lake."

"Fair enough," Celia says. She's already hanging it up again in her closet. "I guess I'm just ready to try something new, you know? A new look and a new...everything."

We're all staring at her by the time she turns back around. Her eyes widen in surprise at the sight of us staring. "What?"

Addie's brow is furrowed in concern. "A new everything? What does that mean?"

Celia lifts a shoulder. "I guess I'm just bored, that's all. I need a change."

I watch her fidget before she heads to her dresser and

starts pulling out drawers. "We all change as we grow up, right? We all evolve. But sometimes in this small town and with our little school, it's like…you can't do that."

She turns to glance at me over her shoulder, and I nod. "Yeah. I get that."

I do get it. I just hadn't realized that Celia felt that way. She's universally beloved by our classmates and seems to fit in wherever she goes. She always seems so sure of herself, I never suspected she wasn't satisfied.

"Does this have anything to do with Heath?" Noelle asks, her eyes narrowed in suspicion.

Celia lifts one shoulder. "Maybe a little."

"Is this because he's with Pamela again?" Addie prods.

"Partly." Celia shrugs again. "I'm just tired of wanting something I can't have."

Noelle jumps in, moving to stand by Celia. "If you really want Heath, then you should make a play for him the next time they break up. You know it's just a matter of time."

Celia winces like she's horrified at the thought.

"Or you could just talk to him, at least," Addie says. "He'd love you if you ever spoke to him, I'm sure of it."

Celia shrugs again. Her smile is more jaded than I've ever seen it. "Yeah, well, I'm starting to think I'm never going to be able to talk to him, let alone flirt with him. And besides, if he hasn't noticed my existence after a lifetime of going to the same school, I don't know if he ever will."

Noelle starts to reassure her, but Celia cuts her off with a shake of her head. "It's okay. Really," she says. "I've just been thinking lately that it's time to move on, that's all." She turns to me and flashes me a big smile. "You've inspired me, actually."

"Me?" My brows arch high in surprise.

She nods. "You and Ryan. The way you've moved past all the preconceived ideas you had about each other. How you're sort of...reinventing yourselves, I guess."

I stare at her in silence because—we're reinventing ourselves? This is news to me.

It's not wrong, necessarily. But I hadn't thought about it like that.

"You have seemed a little different since this all started," Addie says, her gaze thoughtful and fixed on me.

"I have? How?"

Addie shrugs. "I don't know. Lighter, maybe? Happier?"

I blink because her words are unexpectedly jarring. Mainly because I don't think she's wrong. I've *felt* different this past week. Not because I've now been kissed or because people think that I'm dating the star football player. But because...because...

I don't know. I don't know how to explain the change that's been happening inside me. It's like there was some shift inside me after we talked on that island. When I finally admitted to the ugly truth I've been carrying around inside.

Noelle flops onto the bed, but she's staring at me too. I have everyone's attention, it seems. "I think letting go of that anger has been good for you," Noelle says.

Celia and Addie nod.

I find myself nodding too. It *is* anger that I let go of. And not just the anger I'd felt toward Ryan—though it was definitely that, too. But it was also a deeper resentment I hadn't even realized I'd been holding onto. It was anger at the way my mom had to give up her dreams, of how my dad walked out and left us to struggle on our own, of how I've always had to work harder than my classmates.

Letting it out into the open had helped me let it go.

Well, maybe not *let it go*. But it helped me put it in perspective, at least.

I don't know how to explain all that to my friends, though, and this shouldn't even be about me. I turn to Celia and reach for her hand again. "Celia, if you want to reinvent yourself, I think that's awesome. I'm here for it."

She smiles as she glances at the dress in the closet. "Maybe I don't need a complete makeover to do it," she says. "I think just moving on to a new crush would help."

"It'd be a good start," I agree.

"We'll find you somebody new," Noelle promises.

"How?" Addie wrinkles her nose. "We've been going to school with the same group of guys since forever."

"Lakeview High isn't the only school around," Noelle says.

"And then there's college," I add.

Celia arches her brows. "You want me to wait another year before I meet someone new?"

I laugh. "No. I meant you could meet someone when you head to NYU for your marketing club's trip this semester."

"Oh yeah," Addie chimes in. "Your trip is the perfect chance to meet someone new."

"See?" I say. "Senior year is a new beginning for all of us."

"Yeah, okay." Celia's nodding as Noelle hands her a sweater to try on. "Meeting someone new on the trip is a good start." She smiles as she slides the sweater over her head. "And besides, I only have to endure being around Heath for one more year, and then I'm free of him."

Celia and the others keep talking, but I'm stuck in the spot where I've been sitting, stewing over her words.

I never really considered how hard it must be to have a

crush on someone who doesn't see you. Someone who it's painful to be around. So I get why Celia wants Heath out of her life.

One more year, and then I'm free of him.

But I can't help but think that's almost exactly what I'd been thinking a couple weeks ago about Ryan. I'd been counting the seconds until he was out of my life for good. And now?

The thought of him leaving. Of me leaving. Of us not seeing each other ever again...

I grip the arms of the chair I'm on as I battle a wave of panic.

I don't want to never see him again. That much is clear.

But what does that mean? That I want to see more of him? That I don't want to stop seeing him?

I blink as I meet my own wide, horrified eyes in the reflection of the mirror.

Does that mean I want to date Ryan? Like...for real?

Noelle's looking out the window, and she turns to face me with a grin. "Your lover boy's here."

I jump up so quickly I almost knock over the chair. Ryan's here? He's early, which is not like him. My heart leaps into action in my chest like I'm ready to run for my life.

I honestly can't tell if it's excitement or fear.

This new revelation is messing with my head. I need more time to figure out how I feel. What I want.

Who I want.

I stand stock still in the middle of the room. Do I want Ryan?

Even if I want Ryan, would he want me?

A sinking sensation in my chest has me inhaling quickly, like I can fill this sudden void with air.

I need time. I need space. I need to figure out what this crazy rush of emotions means.

But I don't have time because Celia comes up behind me and gives me a little nudge. "Go. Answer the door."

My feet automatically shuffle forward, but my heart races faster and faster with each step down the long hallway and through the wide open foyer.

There is nothing to be so freaked out about.

It's Ryan. I've known him forever. He doesn't terrify me.

But this feeling does.

I try to swallow down this panic, but my heart feels like it's in my throat when I reach for the door handle and throw open the door, and— "Ben?"

Stupid question. It's clearly Ben standing right in front of me. It's Ben, not Ryan.

My heart sinks in my chest. Something in me deflates like a balloon that's been pricked with a pin.

It's not Ryan.

"Hey, Mara," he says. Then he peers past me. "Am I early?"

"I—um—I—" But I have nothing to say. I literally cannot think of a single sentence, and even if I could, I wouldn't be able to get it past this lump in my throat.

If I'd had any doubts before about what I want—about who I want—the question is answered in that moment.

I'm not excited to see Ben. I've never once gotten worked up over anything Ben has done—for better or for worse. I've never wanted to scratch his eyes out when he's said something immature and dumb. But I've also never wanted to kiss him either. Not really. Not in that full body yearning way that scares the crap out of me.

I've never looked at Ben and felt anything more than friendship.

I know that now. I see it. Because now I know what it's like to feel more. And now that I know, there's no going back. I couldn't confuse friendship for something more if I tried.

And then Ben shifts and I see something else. Some*one* else.

Ryan's walking up the path, right behind Ben. His gaze locks on me with a ferocity I can feel in my belly.

"You're in my way," he growls as he moves past Ben.

My lips part, and I know I should tell him he's being rude. He's being so rude—and to Ben, of all people. But I don't speak quickly enough, and then I'm being pulled into Ryan's arms.

His lips close over mine in a kiss that's quick but firm. It's a claim. A branding.

My girl, the kiss seems to say.

He lets me go and I stumble back in time to see Ben ducking his head, his cheeks a little red at the PDA he just witnessed. But then he mumbles something about saying hi to the others and moves past me.

And then it's just me and Ryan. As he stands there watching me with that darkened gaze and a heavy brow, I can only think one coherent thought.

I'd lied to my mom. Ryan *is* the one.

Or he might be.

And nothing has ever scared me more.

SIXTEEN

Ryan

MARA LOOKS like a deer in headlights, and I can't blame her.

I came in hard and fast and didn't give her a second to breathe before I kissed her.

But I couldn't stop myself. She was standing there in bare feet and looking like some summertime goddess...

And she was smiling at the wrong guy.

She'd been gazing up at Ben like he was the only person on the planet. It was jealousy, plain and simple, that had me kissing her. Now that Ben's gone, I feel a jolt of guilt for the caveman move. That's not me. I might be a football star, but I don't go around acting like a jealous brute. At least...I never had before Mara.

She recovers quickly. Of course she does. Nothing sets Mara Loman back for long. "I see we're taking our mission to make Ben jealous very seriously today."

I glare down at her as she pats my arm. "A for effort," she says. "Really."

But she's not quite meeting my eyes, and I can't read her tone, either. I'm pretty sure there's a hint of sarcasm there.

"Isn't that the point of all this?" I ask.

She lifts her gaze then, and for a long moment, she stares straight into me. I wish like hell I knew what she's seeing.

I wish I had any clue what's going on in her head.

But her small smile is crooked when she finally glances away. "So, you ready or what?"

Or what, I want to say. I don't feel like going to a party where we'll be surrounded by people. I want to drag her into my car, take her somewhere private, and spend the rest of the night kissing her until she agrees to be my girlfriend for real.

I take a deep breath. But that's obviously not going to happen. I have mere days left before school starts and she finds out that Leah isn't going anywhere. Maybe less if Leah tells people tonight. I need to use every second I can get to convince her that we could be good.

We could be great.

I snag her hand as I head past her into Celia's house. "Where are your shoes?"

"In Celia's room," she says. "I'll be right back."

This leaves me with time on my hands that I wish I didn't have. I see Ben in the living room, he's sitting on a couch with Addie and Noelle, but I don't go in.

This is it. Tonight is the night. I show her the time of her life. I kiss her until she's jelly in my arms. And then I tell her how I feel.

My heart takes a flying leap toward the front door.

I run a hand over my hair and breathe deep. I can

honestly say I've never been so scared in all my life. If she says no...

If she gives me that wince of regret and backs away...

If she tells me she still has feelings for Ben...

I let out a sharp exhale and force myself to focus. When she comes back out clad in some tennis shoes and with a windbreaker over her arm, I can finally breathe normally again.

I can *focus* too. In fact, she's all I can see as she leads us out the front door.

"Shouldn't you tell Ben you're leaving?" I ask.

I don't know why. Part of me thinks I might be a masochist for bringing him up right now, and I'm sure of it when she glances over. She's not smiling, and for the life of me I can't read her eyes.

"I'll see him there," she says.

Not what I want to hear. But what *do* I want to hear? I guess in my ideal world she'd say *Screw Ben. I don't care if I ever see him again.*

That might be asking for too much.

I'd settle for a *Who's Ben?* Instead. See? I'm mature like that.

"Do you think it's working?" I ask as I help her into the car. "With Ben, I mean."

"I don't know." Her answer is slow, like she's weighing her words. Then she flashes me this bright smile that steals my heart right out of my chest. "I guess I'll find out soon enough."

"So you're gonna go right from my arms to his?" I shake my head. "That's cold, Loman."

She laughs because she knows I'm teasing, but I'm being eaten up inside and her laughter sounds strained. So...great. Excellent start to our first date. Our first *real* date.

Although, she doesn't know it's our first real date. Not yet, at least.

Does it still count as real if she's unaware of the fact that it's real?

Probably not.

When I pull out of the driveway, I head in the opposite direction of the lake, and Mara turns to me in surprise. "Oh, um, shouldn't we be—"

"There's one thing I want to do first," I say. This is a gamble. And I'm not even sure why I'm doing it. To prove something to her or to myself...to both of us, maybe? Mara doesn't say a word until we pull into the parking lot of the country club.

"What are we doing here?" she asks as she follows my lead and unbuckles her seatbelt. "Don't tell me you want to go for a pre-party swim."

I laugh. "Not quite."

I snag her hand when I come around to her side of the car, and that's how we walk into the country club's posh dining room. Hand in hand. "I want you to meet my folks," I say.

She starts to say something, but I don't give her a chance. I know where they're at—my parents are boringly predictable with their routines. And Friday nights always begin with martinis before dinner.

"We don't have to interrupt," Mara's whispering behind me. I ignore her as we come to a stop beside my thoroughly startled parents.

"Ryan," my mom says. "What are you doing here?"

At the same time, my dad smiles at Mara. "Aren't you going to introduce us to your friend?"

Mara stiffens beside me. Out of the corner of my eye, I

see her tight smile. Ever polite, especially in front of parents, she can't scream at me to explain what's going on.

Which is for the best, because I'm not sure how to explain, and my heart is tripping over itself as I say, "Mom, Dad, I just wanted to swing by so you can meet my *girl-friend*, Mara."

Mara's grip tightens to the point that it's painful. Like, I'm pretty sure she's crushing bones. But she maintains that cute little smile as she sticks her free hand out to shake my father's and then returns my mom's awkward hug.

My mom is so embarrassingly excited. My dad too. It's painful, I'll admit it. And it's partly my fault. I've never introduced any girl to my parents before. I've never even been tempted to. And I know it could be a big mistake. I know there's a very good chance Mara is going to break my heart before this night is over and having to explain that she dumped me to my parents will only make it worse.

But this is something I have to do. For me? For her? I don't even know. I just know it feels right even as it makes the pounding in my chest intensify to the point where I'm starting to wonder if cardiac arrest is in my near future.

But soon enough, I see a chance to make our excuses and I seize it. "We're supposed to meet people," I say as I drag Mara away from my mother's death grip.

Mara's silent as I lead her out. Her hand's still in mine. It hasn't left mine since we arrived.

"Sorry about all the hugging," I say when we hit the parking lot. "My mom's always wanted a girl." As if that explains anything. I shrug like it's no big deal when she glances up at me. Like I didn't just set myself up for failure in my parents' eyes when this ends.

If this ends.

I cling to that thought like a lifeline. It might not end. I look over at Mara. I could tell her now, but I'm not sure my heart can handle it. And judging by the little frown of confusion Mara's wearing, I'm not sure she's ready to hear it either.

I open her car door and close it behind her. When I get in the driver's seat, she's watching me. "What was that about?"

I shrug because even if I could explain, I'm not ready to. Explaining this side excursion means opening up a whole can of worms. Or...opening up my heart.

And I will.

I want to.

But first... I glance over at her and take in the new hairstyle, the way her eyes seem to glow with curiosity, and the remnants of shock at what we'd just done. "You ready to have some fun?"

Her lips curve up at the corners, and my heart stops. It just *stops*, and I'm pretty sure time stops right along with it. Then it kicks back into action with a jolt as she reaches out for my hand and links her fingers through mine like it's the easiest thing in the world. Like it's natural and right and...

It is.

"I thought you said I don't know how to have fun," she says as she turns to face forward and I back out of the parking spot.

"I was wrong," I say.

Her gasp is hilariously melodramatic. "Say it again," she insists. "I'm positive I didn't catch that."

I laugh under my breath and stop the car at the exit of the country club. I turn to her with a grin. "I was wrong. And it would seem I've been wrong about a lot of things."

Her eyes are dancing with laughter, but there's a

warmth there that I feel all the way to my bones. "It turns out I've been wrong about a lot of things too."

I mimic her gasp, and she bursts out in a laugh.

"Okay, okay," she says, turning back to look ahead as I pull out onto the road and head toward the lake. "So we've both been wrong. But I am all for putting the past in the past and having some fun."

I grin. "That's what I was hoping to hear."

SEVENTEEN

Mara

IT'S OFFICIAL. I've never had more fun in my life. Music is blaring from speakers someone set up in the parking lot, and I'm laughing so hard I can barely breathe as Ryan spins me into a twirl.

"I thought you said you can't dance," I say as I come to a stop. I'm partially resting against him because he's worn me out with the dancing, but he pulls me in closer so he's taking all my weight, and I'm...I'm...

I'm *happy*.

I am so freakin' happy it hurts. My head's still spinning from the twirling ever since Ryan took my dancing challenge to heart.

To be fair, it was on the scavenger hunt list to make a spectacle at the lake, and judging by the stares we're currently getting, I'd say we succeeded.

"I didn't say I *couldn't* dance," he says. "I said I *don't* dance."

He's smiling down at me, and there's all the cocky arrogance I've come to expect from this guy. But there's also so much more. And the glow from the bonfire makes his always handsome features sharpen with each flickering shadow.

But that's nothing compared to the warmth in his eyes when he smiles at me like this.

He's rocking me in his arms now, back and forth to the music in a sort of middle-school style slow dance as I catch my breath.

"Why don't you dance when you're so good at it?" I pull back slightly to give him an exaggerated frown. "And how *did* you get so good at it?"

His grin turns wicked and all of the sudden he's pushing me out and twirling me around, and then tugging me back. It all happens so quickly, I can only squeak in surprise before I'm back in his arms, my heart racing once more.

He leans his head down until his lips are right next to my ear. "If I tell you how I know how to dance, you've got to promise that it stays between you and me. Our little secret."

I shiver as I nod, a flicker of sensations chasing over my skin at the heady feel of his breath against my ear and the intimacy in his words. "Our secret," I promise.

He pulls back so I can see his eyes and the hint of a smile on his lips. "Dance classes."

I blink. "What?"

He shrugs. "My mom insisted that all of us learn how to dance."

"Like, taking ballet classes to help your football game?" I ask.

"No, like ballroom dancing," he says, his arms tightening around me. "For occasions just like this."

"For bonfires by the lake with your pseudo girlfriend?" I tease.

He lets out a huff of laughter. "For nights when I want to impress a girl."

My breath catches in my throat. He's teasing. I think. But also...he doesn't look like he's teasing. He looks utterly sincere.

He leans down again until his nose brushes against mine. "Is it working?"

I nod, and the movement brings my lips excruciatingly close to his. I lift my arms slightly, and he shifts too so in one seamless move I'm pressed against his hard chest, my arms twined around his neck, and his lips a breath away from mine. "It's working," I say.

His kiss is light and sweet...and just for me.

We're not alone. The rest of our class is loudly partying it up all around us, but nothing about this kiss is for show. It's soft, and it's sweet, and it feels private, even if we are in public.

When he pulls back, my heart is racing. And when he looks down at me, a thrill races through me and leaves me weak. He's looking at me like it's real.

I *feel* like this is real.

But is it?

We haven't talked about the fact that I met his parents. I haven't brought myself to ask what that meant, and he hasn't offered an explanation. Part of me doesn't want to delve into it because I'm a little afraid I'm reading this all wrong.

I pull back slightly as I try to steady my breathing and make my head stop spinning.

Okay, maybe I'm a lot afraid.

I've been coming to grips with the way I feel tonight.

With each new laugh and every unexpected conversation, the realization that I like this guy is settling into place. I'm almost at peace with it—or I would be, if I was sure he felt the same.

But I'm not.

And I wish I were brave enough to outright ask him. But I don't want to ruin this perfect night by finding out he's just having fun until it's over. The way he'd mentioned Ben earlier? Not exactly the comments of a guy who's burning up with desire, now is it?

The thought has me backing up another step. Self-preservation is underrated, in my humble opinion, and right now I feel the need to retreat in a big way. The more I feel for Ryan, the harder it'll be if this ends.

When this ends.

I bite my lip. Oh crap. I shouldn't have started down this mental road. I should have kept kissing him. Kept dancing. I should have just enjoyed one freakin' night without worrying about the future.

But maybe that's just not me.

"You okay?" He kills me when he reaches out to smooth back some of the hair that's escaped from Celia's braided crown.

She and my other friends are in view, and it looks like they're having almost as much fun as me. Ryan follows my gaze, and I see him smile at the sight of Celia and Noelle dancing with abandon as Addie sits on a log nearby watching and laughing.

"I'm keeping you from your friends, aren't I?" he asks.

Yes. "No." Truthfully, I'd been having so much fun with Ryan I hadn't wanted to break it up, not even to hang out with my friends.

Does this make me a bad friend? Maybe.

Probably.

I wince. "I should go check in." I nod toward Addie. "I want to make sure she's having fun. Parties aren't really her thing."

"Right. But you," he teases, stepping in so close it makes my heart leap. "You are such a party animal."

I laugh and it comes out breathless. "You know me."

"Yeah. I do." He sounds way too serious, but then he gives me a gentle nudge toward Addie and the others. "What I know is, you're a really good friend."

My lips part in surprise at the unexpected compliment. But he's already turning away, heading toward his friends who he's been just as neglectful of.

I head over to Addie and sit down beside her. For a little while we watch Celia and Noelle, and we crack up when their impromptu dance-off leads to weirder and funnier dance trends.

"You know you don't have to babysit me, right?" Addie asks after a while.

"I'm not babysitting. I wanted to hang out with you guys."

She smiles and nudges my shoulder with hers. "You're sweet, Mara, but anyone with eyes can see how into each other you guys are. You should go enjoy your night with Ryan."

I shrug but I feel her watching me and when I glance over, she's wearing a knowing smile. Part of me feels like I should remind her that this is just an arrangement. That we have an end date, and that date is looming. Just as soon as Leah leaves town, we'll have no reason to stay together.

But I don't have it in me to argue, and by the way she's looking at me, she wouldn't believe me anyhow.

I wouldn't believe myself.

"So?" She nudges me again. "What are you going to do about it?"

I look across the bonfire to where Ryan's hanging out with his friends and find him staring right back. "I should talk to him," I say.

Addie gives a little snort of amusement. "You think?"

I laugh as she starts to shove me off the log where we're perched. "Go," she says. "I'm fine. We're all good. You go take care of you for once."

The 'for once' hits a nerve for some reason. "What's that supposed to mean?" I say as I stand.

Addie looks up at me with a sigh and a sweet smile. "Just that you spend a whole lot of time worrying about what other people need or want. Your mom, your friends, even Leah and Ryan. It's time you go after what you want."

I nod slowly. "Yeah. Okay."

I turn toward Ryan with my head held high. I learned a long time ago that holding your chin up and keeping your shoulders back is the only way to move forward. I might not feel brave on the inside, but I knew better than anyone how to fake it.

Ryan sees me coming and breaks away from his friends. I try not to do something stupid like shake out my hands and stretch my neck like I'm about to dive into battle.

This isn't battle. It's not a fight. I just need to tell him the truth about how I feel, that's all. When his gaze clashes with mine, I find myself smiling. The way he looks at me—it's so intense it feels like a collision when his eyes meet mine. And how fitting is that? It's always been a clash with us. It always has been, and it likely always will be.

It would probably be easier to pick a fight with him right now than it is to just tell him the truth, but I'm not a coward and I can do this.

"Oops!" Leah bumps into me as she heads toward the other side of the crowd. "Sorry."

Ryan's almost reached me, but Leah's already talking a mile a minute and I can't get away. "...and looks like you guys are having a blast," she says. "And me too. I mean, I'm all out celebrating tonight, so I'm right there with you."

"You're celebrating?" I ask. I'm absurdly aware of Ryan, as if I can feel him as he gets close.

"Yeah, didn't Ryan tell you? I'm staying here for the school year."

I whip my head around to face her. "You are?"

She nods, her smile growing. "I can't believe Ryan didn't tell you. I was sure he had, or I would have waited and told you along with everyone else during my *big reveal*." She throws her arms wide and sort of sings the words *big reveal,* but I'm too stunned to respond. Leah doesn't seem to notice because she's back to talking, all about her plans for the school year and how happy she is to be staying, and—

And Ryan knew. How long has he known?

My head's swimming by the time he reaches my side and wraps an arm around my waist.

"I was just telling Mara how I'm going to be your new classmate this year," she says.

I feel Ryan stiffen, and that makes my stomach sink. For a second there I'd been trying to justify why he hadn't told me that our end date was canceled. That our whole fake-relationship-to-spare-Leah's-feelings plan was a bust. But the way he's tensed beside me, the way he's avoiding my gaze when I look up at him...

He reeks of guilt. My stomach churns as I pull away from him.

Leah's called away by one of her friends, and I'm left alone with Ryan. For a second we stand side by side in silence. The music has gone from fun to grating, and the partying going on around us makes me want to scream. I need a moment of silence to figure this out. To figure out why I feel so uneasy.

Am I being paranoid? Maybe. But if a lifetime of being at odds with Ryan has taught me anything, it's that I can't trust him. Right?

I shake off the thought and take a deep breath. There's probably a simple explanation. I mean it's not like this changes much. It just means we'd have to set a new end date, right? So then...why didn't he just tell me?

"You knew?" I finally ask.

"Only for, like, a day." He says it so quickly, so defensively. It makes my paranoia ratchet up another ten notches, and I find myself thinking of every reason he might have kept this from me.

None of them are good.

When I turn to face Ryan, his expression is unreadable, and with his back to the fire, his face is too shadowed to make out his eyes. I walk away. I know he's following me, and that's fine. That's good. I just need to talk to him somewhere where people aren't dancing around us or shouting to be heard over the music.

When we're far enough away that the music is muffled by the wind and the glow of the fire doesn't reach us, I stop and turn.

"I only knew for a day," he says again before I can speak. His tone is so defensive it borders on aggressive.

It's the look in his eyes that makes me cringe. He's so wary. So angry. It makes me doubt everything I thought I was coming to know about this guy. This truce we've formed feels like nothing compared to a lifetime of being at each other's throats.

How many times has he played tricks on me?

"Why didn't you tell me?" I'm surprised that my voice is so calm, so even.

But that makes his frown deepen and his brows come down in anger. With an ache in my gut, I feel it happening. I *see* it happening.

We're squaring off like we've always done.

"Why?" His smirk makes my insides twist in pain and anger. "Why do you think?"

My brain is racing, trying to understand. If he'd told me, we would have ended this. There'd be no reason to continue.

"I don't know," I say.

He gives a little huff. "Right."

There's a flicker of hope as I wonder if maybe, just maybe he doesn't want this to end either. Maybe we're not on opposite sides here. I take a step forward. "I just don't understand why you didn't tell me right away."

Please tell me it's because you didn't want to let me go. I bite the inside of my lip to stop the words from spilling out. It's too pathetic to say aloud, especially when he's giving me this condescending look like I'm overreacting. Like I'm some uptight, annoying frenemy who he has to put up with.

"Look..." He looks away as he runs a hand through his hair. "I just needed some more time, that's all."

"More time for what?" I ask. Confusion is warring with hope, and it's making my insides feel like they're coming apart.

There's so much I want to say. So much I want to hear. But there's this crushing wave of fear that's overriding everything else, because...what if I'm wrong?

What if I'm alone in this?

What if I'm the idiot who believed our own lies?

He gives an exasperated sigh like he's dealing with a child. "I don't know, Mara." He drops his hand to his side and shrugs. "More time to figure out how to let Leah down easy, I guess."

His tone is all condescending disdain, like I'm making too much out of this. It's the voice he's always used when we fight. It's the voice I've heard my entire life that's always telling me I take everything too seriously. That I don't know how to just let loose and have fun. I don't know how to play games.

And that's what this is, isn't it? A game.

I take a step back as my lungs hitch and my chest tightens painfully.

That's all this is.

I'm trying to keep my cool, I really am. But there's a voice in my head that's howling in pain because...was he just using me? Was he laughing at me?

I don't know. And the fact that I don't know has my arms crossing tightly over my chest like I can physically protect myself from this hurt. "I was bound to find out," I say. "I mean, as soon as I saw her at school on Monday I would have known."

"I know that." His tone has a bite to it. It's all defensive indignation.

"We couldn't keep going on like this indefinitely," I continue. Some part of me is begging him to explain. To give me some explanation that will make everything all right again.

He huffs and looks up toward the sky like I'm trying his patience.

"So why didn't you just tell me?" I ask.

His gaze drops to meet mine so suddenly, my heart gives a little kick at the sudden eye contact. There's a challenge in his eyes. And something else. Something darker. It's anger or it's pain, and I don't know why. "What's this really about, Mara? You pissed that you're missing your big opportunity with Ben?"

"No, that's not—"

"Have at it," he says as he backs away. He throws his arms out wide like he's literally letting me go. "Congratulations, Mara, you're a free woman again."

He turns and walks away before I can respond. And that's probably for the best, because I have no idea what to say.

The sight of him walking away makes my chest feel like it's being severed in two. I clap a hand over my mouth as a sob works its way up my throat and chokes me.

Even if I knew what to say, I wouldn't trust myself to speak.

I've humiliated myself enough by falling for my enemy.

I'm not about to let him see me cry.

EIGHTEEN

Ryan

I HATE MYSELF.

I also hate Mara.

And Ben.

And maybe Leah too.

"You gonna drink that beer, man, or are you just trying to crush the can with your mind?" Heath leans against the truck I'm propped against. I don't even know whose it is, and I don't really care.

I didn't realize I was staring down at the unopened can in my hand until he called me out on it, but I don't move an inch. I also don't respond. Heath doesn't seem to expect me to. That's the nice thing about Heath. He's always down with sitting in silence.

"Wanna talk about it?" he finally asks.

"Not really."

He shrugs. "Fair enough."

Heath makes no move to leave. He's a good friend. Probably a way better friend than I deserve. I scrub a hand over my face as that anger I've been latching onto starts to fade. I don't want it to go. Because the second I stop hating Mara and the rest of the world, I'm gonna be faced with a world of regrets.

Too late. The anger I've been trying to rationalize is disappearing into thin air, and my justifications are just getting lamer by the second.

I groan and drop my head as the reality of what I've just done washes over me.

"Now you ready to talk?" Heath asks. His voice is so mild, like he's cool either way.

"No," I say. And then, two seconds later, I blurt it out. "I screwed up."

He looks over at me with that broody look of his that actually gives away nothing. "So fix it."

I nod, struck for a moment by the sage wisdom in his simple advice. No questions, no rationalizing, just...fix it.

I take a deep breath, and for the first time since I'd walked away from Mara—like a total dumbass, I now realize —I look around at the party that's still raging.

There's no sign of her.

My stomach hits the dirt at my feet, and the mix of regret, shame, and frustration has my gut clenching into a knot. This is exactly why I hadn't looked up in the first place. I hadn't wanted to see that she'd left.

I hadn't wanted to face the consequences of my own actions.

My own stupid, cowardly, asinine actions.

"Why didn't I just tell her the truth?" I say suddenly.

Heath takes a sip of his beer. I guess he realizes it's a rhetorical question and not one that's meant for him.

Why *hadn't* I told her the truth?

Not about Leah. That I knew the answer to. I'd kept my mouth shut because I'd wanted a little more time to try and convince Mara that she might like me.

And that's exactly what I should have told Mara when she'd asked. *I wanted more time with you. I like you. I don't want to let you go.* The words are so simple. Why couldn't I just say them?

Because I'd been too afraid she'd reject me, that's why. I'd taken one look at her self-righteous glare and seen all the years she'd hated me staring me right in the face. In a heartbeat I'd watched it play out in my mind's eye. Me confessing my feelings. Her looking on in horror before pushing me away.

So instead, I'd gotten all defensive, and a lifetime of following the motto *the best defense is offense* had me flipping the switch from idiot-with-a-crush to even-bigger-idiot-with-a-crush-who-hates-him.

"I'm so stupid," I groan.

Heath doesn't argue.

My gaze is still moving over the crowd, but there's no sign of her. I see Celia, Noelle, and Addie, but Mara's not with them.

"I did exactly what she accused me of doing," I say.

Heath's silence makes it easy to say it aloud. All the thoughts that've been racing around in my head as I stood here stewing, trying like hell to be angry at anyone other than myself.

"I'm a coward, and she knows it," I say.

"I've never thought of you as a coward," Heath says, his voice mild.

"Yeah, well..." *You don't know me.* Not the way that Mara does. Heath's a great friend, and I'd do anything for my brothers and the guys on my team, but no one has ever seen through my crap like Mara. She always has. Even when we were eight, she wasn't about to let my bad behavior fly. And as we'd gotten older, she'd only ever seen the worst. The part of myself that I hated, that I hid from the rest of the world.

It's the cowardly part that's so afraid of failing, I never even try.

Mara really nailed it with that one.

I'd known it then, that night at the party when this whole thing began, but it's painfully clear now just how spot-on her take on me had been.

A lifetime of being a success has made me fear failure so much that I don't take chances, I never take risks, and as of today—I don't put my heart on the line.

"I could have just told her the truth," I say. "I could have just told her that the only reason I didn't tell her Leah was staying was because I didn't want us to end before I had a chance to tell her how I feel."

Heath nods as if this makes sense, when it couldn't possibly.

"Instead, I let her believe the worst," I continue, regret making my voice tight. "I let her think I'd just been using her to avoid the inevitable." I turn to Heath as if he can somehow miraculously make this right. "I don't even know why I did it, you know? I don't know why I couldn't just tell her the truth. It's like, one second I was in control, and the next I slipped into some former version of myself that I hate."

"Like a bad habit," Heath says. I catch his gaze roaming over to Pamela who's laughing with her friends. He turns back to me with a grim smile. "I can understand that."

I nod, a humorless laugh slipping out because...yeah. I guess he can.

"But you can still make this right," he says. Heath sounds so confident, it makes me want to believe him. "We all backslide sometimes. We make progress, we make mistakes..." He shrugs and trails off like the rest is obvious, and for a second I find myself wondering when Heath had become our group of friends' very own Yoda.

"The question is, how are you going to move forward?" he asks.

"I don't know, man," I say. "I doubt she'll give me another chance. I mean, I let her think I don't care if she ends up with Ben." I shake my head. "She's probably off with him right now, telling Mr. Nice Guy what an asshat I am."

Heath makes a *hmm* noise as he considers this. "I don't think so."

"No?" I mutter, too miserable to even crack my beer. "Why not?"

Heath nods toward two people who are making out by a tree a little ways down from us. "Because Ben's currently got his tongue down Leah's throat."

I stand up straight for a better look, and— "What the *hell?*"

I say it too loud, but neither of them seem to hear. They're too lost in this hot and heavy makeout session to notice much of anything. Including the fact that they have an audience.

Outrage and relief surge up at once and the result is...confusing. I can't believe I'm actually angry on Mara's behalf.

Had he been leading her on? Did she know? Was she hurt?

But also—*hallelujah.*

I mean, seriously. I stare with wide eyes at the sight

before me. Having Ben out of the picture doesn't necessarily mean that I have a shot in hell. But, even so, at least she's not the one making out with him right now, and that was pretty much my biggest fear.

Heath nudges my arm, and I turn away from the private scene I'm gawking at to look at my friend. "Did you know this was happening?"

He shakes his head. "The more important question is, did Mara?"

I stare at him for a long moment because for a guy who theoretically shouldn't know anything about anything going on between me and Mara, he seems to have gathered quite a bit.

"I don't know," I finally say.

"Well, if she does and she's disappointed, she'll probably need a friend," he says, giving me a pointed look. "And if she's *not* disappointed, that's probably something you ought to know."

I nod, my heart racing in my chest as I get his meaning.

"Either way..." He shrugs. "She probably deserves to know the truth. Don't you think?"

"Yeah." I'm already walking away to find her. "She definitely deserves to hear the truth."

She also deserves an apology.

"Good luck," he calls after me.

"Thanks," I say. "I'll need it."

The fact that her close friends are all at the lake means she's probably still around somewhere. She'd need a ride to leave so odds are she's found a private spot to be alone for a while.

I roam the edges of the party for ten minutes before I catch sight of her. She's gone past the treeline and into the woods, but not far. Ever practical, she's stayed close enough to the action for safety's sake and far enough away for some privacy.

She's sitting on a big rock, and when I get close, she jumps up with a start.

I hold my hands up and realize that she can't see me since I'm backlit by the fire. "It's just me," I say.

I hear her exhale. I'd like to say it's a sigh of relief, but I'm pretty sure it's disappointment. Had she hoped I was Ben? I wince at the thought.

"What do you want?" she asks. But despite the not-so-friendly words, her voice lacks heat. She sounds...tired. And that makes my chest ache all over again.

I stop when I get close enough that she can see me, and I can make out the look in her eyes. It's wariness. But not hate. Not even anger.

I have no idea what to say. I should have prepared. In my defense I'd thought this whole confession moment would come about while we were making out in my car, maybe with some music playing and definitely when she's looking all dazed and sweet in my arms. I don't know where to start, so I just open my mouth and say the only thing I can think of.

"I lied." The words tumble out a little too loudly, and her eyes widen in response.

"What?" she says.

I nod toward the place we were standing by the bonfire. The place where we'd danced and laughed and kissed and— "Do you really think I'm doing all this because of Leah?"

She blinks in surprise.

I run a hand through my hair. I'm supposed to be wooing the girl, not yelling at her. But I'm frustrated. With myself, mainly, but also with her. Because she'd leapt to the worst conclusion about me. Again. And I hate how much that hurts.

But also, why should she trust me?

And why should she believe a word I'm about to say when I've done what I always do. I took the easy way out.

"What did you lie about?" she asks. Once again, she looks and sounds wary. Like she's not sure if she can trust me.

"I didn't tell you about Leah staying because I didn't want *this* to end right away," I say, gesturing between us. "But not because I'm putting off an awkward conversation with Leah, and not because I'm trying to mess with you and Ben."

She shifts, folding her arms across herself as she bites her lip. "Then why?"

"Because I like you, Mara," I say. The moment it's out, it's such a relief, I don't even care that her only response is to widen her eyes in shock.

The truth coming out feels like a giant wedge being unstuck from my throat, and now it's coming out in a current of words. "I like you a lot. And I like you as more than a friend." Just in case there was any confusion. "I was going to tell you about Leah. And of course I knew you'd find out sooner rather than later. But I wanted to show you first." I stop to take a deep breath. "I wanted to show you that we could be great together."

The silence that follows just about kills me.

It's filled with the music and laughter of the party behind me, but here in these woods we might as well be on a different planet. And in this world, I might just suffocate on all the tension that fills the silence between us.

"You—you *like* me?" Her voice is so tentative and soft.

So not like Mara. It makes me want to scoop her up in my arms and hold her tight.

"I do," I say instead, stepping closer so maybe I can feel what she's feeling or at least see what she's thinking. "I'm sorry I lied. I have no excuse. You were pissed, and I just—" I shrug. I don't want to rationalize anymore. I don't want to justify. "I'm working on it," I say instead. "I'm working on facing failure and owning up to my mistakes."

Her lips part, and she's so perfectly kissable right now it's insanely hard not to tug her into my arms.

"I'm not there yet," I say. "But I'm trying. And that's all because of you."

I take another step closer and touch her cheek to swipe away a tear that nearly breaks my heart. "I don't expect you to feel the same way about me just yet. I know this is all happening quickly and you don't have any reason to trust me, but I—"

"Wait." She holds a hand up in my face like a traffic cop. "Ryan, just...wait."

I freeze.

Then she's up on her toes and she's pressing her lips to mine in a fierce kiss, that's almost like our very first kiss, except that this time I don't waste a second before burying my hands in her hair so I can kiss her back with all the love that's in my heart.

NINETEEN

Mara

I HAVE no idea what my heart is doing, but I think it's trying to escape. It's beating so hard and so fast, and all I can do is kiss Ryan like my life depends on it.

It kinda feels like it does.

His mouth is hot and urgent as he takes control of the kiss and crushes me to him. Relief floods through me, washing away the pain I've been drowning in ever since he walked away.

But the regret and the shame? They're still there. I pull back and press my hands to his shoulders when he leans in to kiss me again. "Wait," I pant as I try to catch my breath. "I have to tell you something too."

His arms tighten around me, but he doesn't move. The expression in his eyes is so freakin' sweet. It's so vulnerable, and the fact that I'm quite possibly the only person on the planet who knows how hard that is for him... My heart clenches with emotion.

"I'm sorry," I whisper.

He kisses my forehead as I take a deep breath to continue.

"I'm sorry," I say again, louder this time. "I did the same thing as you. I slipped back into my old ways. I assumed the worst, and I'm sorry."

"You've already said that." He's wearing this small, crooked smile that makes my heart thud against my ribcage. "And it's okay. You have good reasons not to trust me—"

"No, but that's the thing. I do trust you." I take another deep breath and slide my hands up to clutch his shoulders, like I can steal some of his strength. "I do trust you. I think I just got...scared." The word is hard to get out and judging by his knowing smile, he totally understands that. "I got scared and my first instinct was to defend myself. I guess it's just easier to get angry than—"

"To risk getting hurt?" He drops a quick, hard kiss on my lips before he says, "Yeah. I totally get that."

"But I overreacted," I say. "I leapt to conclusions, and I didn't give you the benefit of the doubt, and I really am sorry."

"I'm sorry too," he says. After a beat he pulls back to meet my gaze head-on. "Hey, Mara?"

"Yes?"

"Can we go back to kissing now?"

I burst out into a laugh. "Yes. We should definitely—"

He claims my lips in another kiss before I can even finish. And for a long moment, I am completely content to shut my brain down and let our actions speak for us. His arms are strong and tight, his lips fierce and urgent. The way he kisses me is the perfect mix of sweet tenderness and unbridled passion, and if that doesn't describe Ryan and our newfound relationship, then I don't know what does.

He scoops me into his arms at one point and sits down on the boulder, settling me in his lap before he goes back to kissing me, his hands exploring my neck, my jaw, my cheeks. When he moves his lips to trail a line of kisses down my jaw and to my neck, he murmurs into my ear. "Now *this* is what I had in mind for tonight."

I smile as a shiver races through me. "You did?"

He nods and pulls back to drop a light kiss on the tip of my nose. "I had this plan to kiss you until you were putty in my arms, and then you'd be helpless to resist when I then explained to you that I wasn't about to let you go."

The breath leaves my lungs in a whoosh at the sincerity in his voice. "You weren't?"

His laugh is low and soft next to my ear. "I have no intention of letting you go. Ever. I wasn't sure if you were ready to hear that, but I was willing to wait." He pulls back to meet my eyes. "I still am. If you're not sure, we can take this slow. I don't want to rush—"

I cut him off with a kiss just like he'd done to me. When I pull back, I meet his gaze. "You're not rushing me. I'd already realized that I like you." I wrinkle my nose because that doesn't sound right. "I mean, I *like* you in the more than friends way."

He's laughing as he pulls me in closer so I'm tucked against him like I was meant to fit into his arms. "I knew what you meant. And I am so freakin' happy to hear you say that."

I smile against his neck as he strokes my back.

"Especially because..." He stiffens beneath me and I pull back to look at him.

"What is it?"

He winces. "I think maybe Ben and Leah are a thing?"

He honestly phrases it like a question, like he's so very

wary of how I'm going to take that. After a heartbeat in which I fully register what he's saying, my head falls back as I let out a loud laugh. "Seriously?"

His grin is sweet and filled with relief. "I saw it with my own two eyes."

My jaw is hanging open in awe as I shake my head in disbelief. "It's perfect," I say.

He starts to laugh, and I know he gets it. They might be the two nicest people we know. "It kind of is, isn't it?"

I tilt my head to the side. "Did you honestly think I was going to be upset to hear that?"

He shrugs, and I feel a tug in my chest at the flicker of vulnerability I see in his eyes. He's still uncertain. Of me. Of *us*.

And I can't blame him because as happy as I am, I feel it too. That sensation of standing at the brink, of getting ready to take a giant leap into the unknown. I swallow hard and lean forward until my forehead rests against his and our breathing mingles. "I'm scared," I admit.

And just saying it aloud takes away some of the fear.

"I'm scared too," he says.

We sit there in silence for a while, listening to the music in the distance and the shouts of laughter from our friends. Ryan touches my chin, and I lean back so see him looking more serious than I've ever seen him before. "But we're in this together, Mara."

I nod, a surge of emotions making it hard to talk. My eyes are welling with tears again, but this time they're tears of relief, and happiness...and maybe even love.

I take a deep breath and link my hands behind his neck. "So we're, like, on the same team?"

I arch a brow and he laughs. "I guess so."

"Huh." I pretend to think that over. "Me and Ryan Hunter. Teammates."

He nods slowly, going along with my teasing with a smirk that makes my belly flip in the best possible way. "Someone ought to warn the rest of the world we're coming."

I laugh. "I'm pretty sure together we're unstoppable."

He's still grinning when he leans in to kiss me. "All I know is, I'd much better be on your side than stand against you."

"Damn straight," I mutter, but then he kisses me so thoroughly I forget who we're trash talking or why.

Not that it matters. After all, we're two incredibly competitive people in one couple...

Something tells me there'll be plenty more where that came from.

EPILOGUE

One year later...

Ryan

WE'RE STANDING in the shallow end of the country club's pool, and I take Mara by the shoulders like I'm her coach. "You ready, babe?"

She nods as she swipes some water from her eyes. Mara's so freakin' hot when she's soaking wet.

Okay fine, she's hot all the time, in my opinion. But right now, in her no-nonsense lifeguard swimsuit and with that look of determination on her face?

Yeah. I'm glad as hell that this girl is mine.

"Ready," she says.

I help her get onto the giant inflatable duck, and she narrows her eyes at me as the rest of the staff members shout out encouragement to the racers heading back our way. "You aren't going to let me win, are you?"

She sounds so suspicious, it's impossible not to laugh. "Of course not."

She rolls her eyes, but a smile teases her lips. "That's what you always say."

It's true. We race a lot. We've also found a whole lot of new ways to compete. And yeah, sometimes I let her win. Sometimes she lets me win too, though, so you know—I'm not the only cheater around here.

I put a hand to my heart. "I promise."

She's laughing as she watches me struggle to get atop my own floatie. A unicorn. And yeah, it's super manly. Her teammate reaches her first, and she's off like a flash.

Don't ask me how, but my girl even manages to make duck riding look hot. She's amazing like that.

When I get to the other end, she's already there, and she's gloating like nobody's business.

"I won!" Her teammates are going wild as they help her out, and she does her happy dance.

It's a ridiculous dance, for the record. But Mara owns it, and my heart is full to the point of breaking as I watch her shimmy around with her teammates.

She's back to gloating next to me soon enough though, and when her arms wrap around my waist and she beams up at me with all that love and laughter and joy... I can't bring myself to care that I lost.

And I won't even tell her later how I let her win.

I'm kind of an awesome boyfriend like that.

"You did your best, sweetie," she says in a cute, if slightly condescending tone as she drops a kiss on chest.

I growl as I wrap my arms around her and steer her backwards until we're apart from the crowd. "Congratulations," I say as I kiss my way from her shoulder to her neck.

She squirms when I hit the spot that always makes her

shiver, and I smile against her skin. "You did great out there."

"And you let me win," she says. But her voice is filled with laughter, so I'm pretty sure she doesn't really care.

Still. I'm not about to admit to it. Not yet, at least.

I kiss her instead, my lips teasing hers in a slow, seductive kiss that's a promise for all that's in store tonight.

Her eyes are gorgeously dazed in that way I love when I pull back to gaze down at her.

"Games are about to start," I say. "You want to play?"

She arches a brow. "That depends. What's the prize if I win?"

I laugh at the reminder of our first kiss. Hard to believe that's how all this began. Who would have thought that I'd find the love of my life thanks to one stupid dare?

She links her fingers through mine with a sweet smile. "I think I might skip the games tonight. I want to get as much time with our friends as we can."

I nod as I wrap an arm around her waist and kiss the top of her head. "Let's get showered and changed then so we can meet up with them at the lake."

I reluctantly let her go, and we say our goodbyes to the other staff members before heading out. We're both quiet on the drive to the lake.

I don't know about Mara, but I keep thinking about last year at this time when we were at the bonfire. The night that changed both our lives.

Since then, we've been a team. A team that loves to compete with one another. A team that loves to make out even more. But a team nonetheless.

Mara's been good for me, no doubt about it. My parents adore her like I knew they would. My brothers too. Everyone can see that she's helped me to be a stronger man.

A bigger man. The kind of man who takes risks and who faces challenges head-on. The kind of guy who loves with all his heart, even if that means being vulnerable.

And I'd like to think I'm good for Mara too. I've made it my mission in life to make sure she doesn't work herself into an early grave, as her mom puts it. I love that she's so driven and I've never been prouder of anyone in my life than I was when she got the scholarship she'd been after. But I figure it's my job to make sure she's having some fun along the way too.

Good thing for both of us I'll be going to school within an hour of her university, so we can keep being there for each other as we head into the next stage. But for now, for tonight...

I reach for her hand and she twines her fingers through mine as we head toward the lake where our friends are waiting. Our days in this town are numbered, and none of us are eager to say goodbye, even though we're all excited to see what the future holds.

Mara's phone dings with a text. "It's Celia," she says. "She just got there."

"Which means Heath must be there already too." I flash her a knowing grin. "I'm still not sure I'm used to this new and improved Heath, you know."

She laughs. "You miss the old brooding Heath?"

"Nah, of course not. But I'm still getting used to seeing him smiling so much."

Mara settles back in her seat with a happy sigh. "All of us have changed so much. It's hard to believe how much can change over the course of one year."

I nod. "And it all started with us."

She gives a little snort of amusement. "I'm not sure we can take credit for everyone else's newfound happiness."

I shoot her a smirk. "I'm just saying, we were the first to fall in love."

She meets my smirk with a cute little grin. "I do love you, Ryan Hunter."

I squeeze her hand, already itching to get there so I can pull her into my arms for a thorough kiss. "But not as much as I love you."

She laughs as I knew she would. "I can't believe you're still trying to win *that* competition."

I shrug, totally unrepentant. "Get used to it, babe. I plan on arguing with you on this point for a very long time."

For the rest of our lives, if I have my way.

But you know, no rush. We're young. We've got time. And until then? We pull into the parking lot of the lake and I give in to temptation and steal a kiss.

Until then, I plan on enjoying every second with the woman I love.

THANK YOU FOR READING! Were you wondering how Leah and Ben got together during all this? I was too! (Okay, fine. Maybe it was just me.) Either way, turn the page to read two bonus scenes from their points of view. I couldn't let this story end without giving these two their own happily ever after!

BONUS SCENES: LEAH & BEN

Leah

One day before the bonfire...

I love having a secret. Or *secrets*, plural.

I have a lot of them.

But as I watch Ryan and Mara sizing each other up on the basketball court, I'm starting to wonder if I'm not the only one.

I like to think I'm good at reading people, but these two are tough. One second, I'm convinced they're madly in love, and the next—like right now—I wonder if they've even met. They're acting all weird over who's going to give Mara a ride to work, which is just...well, *weird*.

Ben looks to me and I wonder if he's as weirded out as I am by the weirdness going on in front of us.

"I didn't know you were going to wait," Mara says. And the way she's looking at Ryan right now?

Awkward.

I back up a step because I feel like I'm intruding on a

couple moment, and I hate that. And it's not just these two. I might have had a crush on Ryan, but I meant it when I'd said I was happy for him and Mara. So no, it's not them in particular. I just hate couple moments in general. Good, bad, or incredibly awkward, like this particular moment I'm witnessing.

Maybe I'd have a different opinion if I'd ever actually been *in* a couple. But when you're always on the outside looking in? Not fun.

"It's fine if you want to go with Ryan," Ben says to Mara. "I was going to head to the lake anyway, and that's the other direction."

I perk up. "I was going to go to the lake too!"

"You need a ride?" Ben asks.

"I'd love that." I'm more than a little relieved to have an excuse to leave these two to whatever is happening here. Maybe they got in a fight or something?

Whatever. All I know is, the two of them have this crazy connection—a visible, palpable energy field tying them together—and I'd pity the fool caught in between.

"Who are you meeting up with at the lake?" I ask Ben as I fall into step beside him on the way to his car.

He gives me a sidelong glance, and the way his lips quirk up on one side takes me by surprise. It's a smirk that's filled with mischief. "You, hopefully."

I would say it's an evil grin if I thought for one second this guy had it in him to be evil. He doesn't. Ben's been hanging out with me and my cousin Elijah all summer, and he might be the nicest guy I've ever met. Not over-the-top gregarious or sweet in an ingratiating way. He's just genuinely nice. And nice is way underrated in my book.

But even so, that flash of wicked mischief fills me with a surge of something warm and light, like fizzy bubbles in my bloodstream. I loop my arm through his as we draw near his car and give it a squeeze. "I'd love to hang out. But if you weren't planning on meeting up with people at the lake, does that mean..." I glance back toward Mara and Ryan.

"I lied." Ben laughs softly. "I just needed an excuse to get out of Ryan's crosshairs."

My head falls back with a much louder laugh. "He did look pretty pissed to see you two together."

"I know, right?" He shrugs and the movement tugs on my arm. "I never would have guessed Mara would fall for a guy who's so...so..."

"Possessive?" I offer.

He flashes me a smile. "Exactly."

"Me neither." I hug his arm because I'm swooning a little on the inside at the memory of the dark intensity in Ryan's eyes just now as he'd looked at Mara. "It's sweet though, don't you think?"

Ben shrugs. "I guess."

Something in his tone has me looking closer. I bite my lip because I'd had a suspicion about Ben this summer. And right now? I'm afraid I was right. "Ben, did you..." I trail off when he glances over at me. "I mean, it's none of my business, but did you have feelings for Mara?"

Ben's brows draw down and his gaze goes all distant and thoughtful.

Thoughtful—that's another trait I'd use to describe Ben. He's thoughtful when it comes to other people's feelings, but he's also thoughtful about *everything*. He's the kind of guy who thinks before he speaks.

So, basically the exact opposite of me in that sense. But I like that about him. I wait patiently for him to think over his response as we climb into his car and buckle our seatbelts.

It's not until we're on the road and heading toward the lake that he responds. "I thought for a little while there that maybe there was something going on between us."

I turn to face him and find myself studying his profile. He's surprisingly handsome in an understated kind of way. The earnestness in his expression right now is endearing, too. It makes me smile just to watch him being so sincere as he sorts through his thoughts and feelings.

"It's not like she led me on or anything," he says, his tone defensive on Mara's behalf. "But we have a lot in common, and we have a good time together, and I guess maybe I read more into it than was really there."

I nod. "Trust me, I totally get that."

He flashes another smile in my direction and I stare in surprise because I'd never noticed before how much a smile transforms this guy's features. For a second there, when his gaze met mine and he was smiling...*whoa.*

He was seriously cute. Not just handsome, but hot. Sexy, even.

I blink a few times as I realize that my heart was beating a little faster for it. Crap on a cracker, is this attraction?

The thought leaves me temporarily speechless, which is a rarity for me, I'd be the first to admit. But Ben's not done talking so he doesn't seem to notice. "And don't get me wrong," he's saying. "I still like Mara. As a friend, I mean. But as soon as I saw her and Ryan together, it clicked. Whatever connection she and I might have, it's not even close to what they share. You know?"

He glances over at me and I nod eagerly, the temporary bout of shock fading as I lean forward with excitement. He *gets* it. "Yes!" I say. He doesn't flinch at my enthusiasm, which is nice. Sometimes even Elijah seems overwhelmed by my naturally high level of energy and he's my best friend as well as my cousin. "That's it exactly," I say. "I feel the same way about Ryan."

"You do?" He arches his brows in question as he looks over.

I get his doubt. Elijah was just as wary of my easy acceptance of Ryan and Mara after hearing me go on all summer about my crush on him.

But Ben said it perfectly. All I can do is repeat it back to him. "I thought Ryan was so perfect for me because...well, because he's hot." I laugh at myself and Ben grins as he watches the road. "And not just that. I mean, I like talking to him, and he's always so nice. But, yeah. One glimpse of him and Mara together and it was so obvious that he and I do not have that sort of spark. Or *any* spark."

Ben shoots me a sympathetic little grimace, and I know he gets it. It's a little embarrassing to admit how wrong I'd been, but then again...we both made the same mistake, so that makes me feel better. "I guess maybe I've never had that with anyone," I say slowly. "So how was I supposed to know the difference, you know?"

He nods, his hands shifting on the wheel as he navigates the traffic to turn off for the lake. "Exactly. I'm honestly grateful that they figured it out so you and I didn't waste any more time crushing on the wrong people."

I grin, leaning back in my seat. I like the way he included me in that statement. Like he'd been worried for my sake too.

He's so freakin' *nice.* My heart clenches with gratitude and appreciation. After the year I'd had at my last school, his kindness feels like balm on the invisible scars I'd been trying so hard to hide.

He looks over and his brows come down in concern at whatever he sees in my expression. "You okay?"

I don't answer. But I do shift in my seat to face him as he pulls into the parking lot. "You're a really nice guy, you know that, right?"

"Thanks."

I didn't miss his wince. It was subtle but I'd seen it. I reach a hand out and touch his arm as he goes to turn off the car. "That's not a bad thing."

My voice is teasing and he turns to me with a grudging smile. "I know."

"Do you?"

He meets my gaze evenly and my smile starts to fade because...this is weird. Not awkward. But tense. The silence feels heavy and I don't know what that means. Or if it means anything at all.

I break the moment by turning to open my car door and get hit with a wave of hot and humid air as I do. We climb out and head toward the pier where our friends normally hang out when there's nothing else going on.

No one's there except for a family with a bunch of little kids.

"Should I call Elijah?" I ask. I don't know why I'm asking. It's not like I need Ben's permission to call my cousin.

"Nah," he says. He doesn't explain, and I don't ask. I love my cousin, and I know Ben's tight with him, so it's not that we don't want to see Elijah or any of the other guys he hangs out with. It's just...

This is nice. I've hung out with Ben a ton this summer but never alone like this. I like it, even though there's a tension I can't really explain that's making me feel weirdly aware of my every move.

I glance over as we make ourselves comfortable on the sand. Does he feel it too?

He seems content to sit in silence and stare out at the lake, but that's not really my thing. I chew on my bottom lip and order myself to be quiet. I know a lot of people don't like it when I talk all the time. I try my best to keep silent, but after about two seconds, I hit my limit and words start spewing out of my mouth like a broken faucet.

I'm telling him all kinds of stuff—but not my big secret. I want to tell him. And maybe I will. But by telling Ryan I'd already broken my vow to myself to keep this a secret until school actually starts.

Call me superstitious but I'm afraid I'll jinx myself if I tell the world I'm staying. It's almost too good to be true that Elijah and his parents made this happen, and if it falls through...

I shake my head and focus on the stupid story I'm telling him about my trip to the mall with Bethany and Bianca the other day.

I can't think about this not working out. Not now when I'm here and I'm happy.

Ben's low laughter when I hit the punchline of my silly story is gratifying. I take a deep breath. I always know I've been talking too much and too quickly when I leave myself winded. "Sorry," I say with a sheepish grin. "I get a little carried away talking sometimes."

"Are you kidding?" Ben sounds so shocked, I look over with arched brows. He leans into me, and his smile is so sweet and so sincere it makes my heart trip in my chest. "I love listening to you talk."

I blink. And then I blink again. "You do?"

His head bobs as he nods eagerly. "Of course. You have so much energy and enthusiasm, it's...it's..."

"Exhausting," I say, automatically filling in with the word that my father uses.

Ben stops nodding to stare at me. "No, not exhausting. It's exhilarating."

I can only sit there and stare because he's obviously teasing. Right?

Wrong. He looks more earnest than ever as he leans in again, shifting so he's right up against me. "Honestly, Leah, your smiles and your laugh and the way you're so passionate and enthusiastic about everything, it's just...it's so refreshing."

"Refreshing?" I sound like I don't understand the English language. Like I'd never heard this word before.

"Yeah, you have so much passion, and it's contagious."

I start to laugh because I've never heard myself described like this, and it's kind of awesome. "Contagious, huh? Sounds like I have a sickness."

His smile is adorable. "If you're sick, I hope I catch it." He dips his head as soon as the words are out. "Wow, that was super lame, right?"

His ears are red and my heart gives another squeeze.

"That wasn't lame at all," I say. "That might just be the nicest thing anyone's said to me." I nudge his shoulder. "*You're* nice."

"Nice." He sort of mutters it under his breath, like he's saying it to himself as he kicks the toe of his shoe into the sand.

"Yes, nice," I say. I feel like I should say more, but I don't know what. I have this urge to tell him how sexy it is that he's nice.

And he is sexy right now, there's no doubt about it. The way his smile makes his eyes crinkle. The way he makes me feel so appreciated and special. The way his gaze is so soft with kindness when he looks at me.

That is so freakin' hot I can't take it.

But I can't say that because if all goes according to plan and my dad doesn't change his mind, I'll be going to school with Ben come Monday. We'll see each other all the time, and I don't want to ruin what might be the first real friendship I've found in Lakeview—aside from my cousin, of course.

"I'm glad we're hanging out alone today," I say instead.

"Yeah?" He peeks over at me, his eyes dark and focused on me like I'm the only person in the world.

Freakin' sexy.

I nod, swallowing hard. "I'm so glad that I made a friend here in Lakeview."

He gives a little huff of laughter. "You have lots of friends here."

"Do I?" It sort of slips out, but it's a genuine question. The people here are nice to me, but I'm pretty sure that's because everyone loves Elijah and he's my cousin. Now that I'm staying, I'm starting to fear that friend-by-association status won't translate to real friendships.

I'm terrified my experience at Lakeview High will be a repeat of my last school.

"You seem to," Ben offers, a question in his eyes.

I force a smile. "I hope so."

I hope things are different here than at home. I hope for that so much it makes my stomach twist painfully.

"Hey." He reaches out and touches my hand, which rests between us on the sand. "You okay?"

My heart stops when I meet his gaze. So genuine. So concerned. So *nice*. When my heart starts again, it kicks in with a jolt, and I swear I can feel it slam against my ribcage. I nod quickly to alleviate the concern in his eyes. "I'm good."

His smile is slow and sweet. "Good."

We go back to staring at the lake, and this time I'm able to sit in silence. And it's so freakin' nice. After a while I rest my head against his shoulder with a contented sigh.

"Am I boring you?" he asks. His voice holds a teasing note as he leans his head to the side so he sort of nuzzles my hair. "I know I can be too quiet sometimes."

"I'm more than capable of making up for your silence," I say with a self-deprecating laugh. I reach a hand up and squeeze his arm. "And no, I'm not bored. Being here with you like this, it's nice. It's..." *Perfect.* "It's...soothing."

<hr>

Ben

Soothing. *Soothing?* Seriously, what am I—a pacifier? A blankie?

The word has been haunting me for twenty-four hours. I'm officially obsessed. I should let it go. I know Leah wasn't trying to offend me.

I stare at my reflection in the mirror over Celia's sink. We're all about to leave for the bonfire, but I can't see Leah again until I get my head on straight.

Soothing. I say the word to myself one more time as I take a deep breath and stretch out my neck, attempting to lower my shoulders as I straighten my spine. So she thinks I'm soothing. So what? There are worse adjectives out there. And again, it wasn't like Leah had been *trying* to insult me.

She would never intentionally hurt anyone. That's the thing about Leah that's so amazing. She's so freakin' sweet. And that sweetness is so incredibly sincere.

And...I like her.

I meet my own stare in the mirror as I take in a deep breath. Wow. Okay, yeah. I'm actually admitting this.

I like Leah. I like her a lot. I think maybe I've had a little crush since the first time I met her at the end of last summer when she was visiting. But I knew even then that she'd been into Ryan and this summer I'd thought maybe something was brewing with me and Mara, and—

And I'm an idiot.

I press my lips together and give my head a shake as I regard my reflection. I've had more fun hanging out with Leah this summer than I've ever had in my life. I've had more fun than I even knew was possible.

My family likes to tease me about being an old man in a teenager's body. They say I take everything too seriously and that I don't know how to lighten up and have fun. And up until Leah came along, I would have said they were right. But it's impossible to be around Leah and not feel lighter...happier. I wasn't exaggerating when I'd said her energy was contagious.

I'm infected with her enthusiasm every time she's around. And that's not the only effect she has on me. My hands are getting clammy just thinking about her, and the collar of my button-down shirt feels too tight.

She's so pretty. I knew this all along but being so close to her yesterday just about killed me. I'd wanted to reach out and touch her. I'd wanted to kiss her.

Why hadn't I?

Because I'm so freakin' nice, I suppose. So very *soothing.*

I lean forward on the counter and take another deep, steadying breath. Frustration has me gripping the edge of the counter hard as I glare at my reflection. "So, what now, idiot?"

My reflection doesn't answer. How do I get Leah to see me as something other than a nice shoulder to lean on? I'm pretty sure I'm firmly in the friend zone, but I have no idea what to do about it.

Worst of all, she'll be leaving soon. I have maybe a week tops to convince her that I'm not some asexual wuss. I'm pretty sure that's what she sees when she looks at me.

I hear the others in the living room, talking loudly and laughing. We'll be heading out any second now and I need a plan. My pulse is elevated when I go to join the others. I'm nervous and excited and—maybe I'm a little terrified too.

But tonight might be my last chance and I'm not going to let it pass without making some sort of move. I just don't know what. Or how.

"You ready, Ben?" Addie asks.

She's looking at me expectantly and I glance around to see that everyone is here except for Mara and Ryan. "Where'd Mara go?"

"She and Ryan took off already," Noelle says.

I nod as Celia goes over the game plan of who's riding with who. But all the while I'm thinking about Ryan and Mara. I'd meant it when I'd said I wasn't upset that Mara chose Ryan.

I like Mara but seeing her with Ryan, it's so clear that we never would have worked. They're so good for each other. They fit in a way that's obvious once you see them together. And if Mara works so well with Ryan then clearly she wouldn't do well with me because Ryan and I are complete opposites. By nature I'm unassuming and quiet. I'm not some alpha jock who needs to be the center of attention, like Ryan.

But Ryan's the one who got the girl.

The thought takes hold and won't let go as I drive Celia

and Noelle to the lake. They're talking and laughing, but all I can do is think about how maybe I've been going about this all wrong.

Maybe if I want to get a girl to notice me I need to stop acting like...well, *me*.

Honestly, the only guys I know who are successfully in committed relationships aren't what anyone would call 'nice guys.' Ryan's not a *bad* guy, and neither is Heath. But I can't imagine either of them being stuck in the friend zone. Ever.

By the time Leah arrives with Elijah, I have a plan. Is it a good one? I don't know. But my time is running out and now that I know I like Leah, I can't un-know it. And I don't want her to leave without her knowing it too.

"Leah, hey," I say when she dances up to me as soon as the music starts.

I can't fight this grin even though I'm pretty sure it's the definition of dopey. I can't help it. She's so stinkin' cute when she's bopping around to the beat, seemingly unaware that no one else has started dancing yet.

"Ben, I'm so glad you're here!" She throws her arms around my neck and I wrap mine around her waist, warning my body and my heart not to read too much into it. Leah's a touchy-feely person by nature. She'll greet everyone at this party with the same effusive hug, mark my words.

Still, the feel of her in my arms makes my chest feel too tight and the urge to tug her even closer has my hands clenching against her back.

I want to kiss her. But not now. Not here. Anyone could see us and she might be horrified. The thought has me even more quiet than usual as she pulls back, chattering a mile a minute about her plans for the night and some exciting news that she can't wait to tell me.

I don't respond appropriately. How can I when all I can

do at this particular moment is stare at her lips and wonder how they'd feel pressed to mine?

"Ben?" Her head tilts to the side. Her eyes are bright and filled with more kindness than I can stand. How could anyone *not* fall head over heels for this girl? She's basically an angel.

And I want her so badly it hurts. I want her in every way possible. I want to be the guy she talks to all night long. I want to be the guy at her side holding her hand when she's having fun or when she's having a bad day. I want to be the shoulder she cries on and the first person she calls when she has good news.

I want to be the guy who kisses her until her eyes are dazed and she forgets how to speak.

I want it all.

But that look in her eyes right now? It screams *friend*. I draw in a deep breath and remember my promise to myself. I'm not going to let this moment pass. I'm not going to let her slip through my fingers—

"Go out with me," I say suddenly. Okay, demand is more like it. It comes out as a harsh command, and she blinks up at me in surprise.

"What?"

I take her hand and tug her away from the crowd. When we're on the outskirts of the crowd, near the trees and out of the fire's glow and warmth, I stop and face her.

"Before you leave, Leah. *Go out with me.*" Yup. That definitely came out as a growl. What am I doing? Am I seriously *demanding* that this sweet girl go out on a date with me? I can barely hear the music that's blaring from a nearby speaker. The booming bass has nothing on my heart right now. It's thudding so loudly, all I can hear is the rush of blood past my ears.

Her lips tremble in an uncertain smile. "What?" She gives her head a shake, and I try not to back down instantly.

Crap. I'm not cut out to be this guy. I'm not some alpha dude who makes demands. This isn't me. A wave of self-loathing hits me hard and my brain flails trying to find a way to make this right.

Her brows draw together in confusion. "You want to go out with me? Like, on a date?"

I consider pulling her in for a kiss, but I can't do it. Already that wave of confidence is passing and I'm a jerk for the way I asked her out. She deserves better.

I clear my throat. "Can I, uh...Can I try this again?"

Her smile is blindingly brilliant. "There's my Ben."

Now it's my turn to blink in surprise. "What?"

Even in this dim lighting I can see her cheeks turn pink. "Sorry. Not *my* Ben, obviously. I just meant, for a second there, you didn't sound like yourself." She bites her lip. "You didn't look like yourself either." She draws her brows down into a mock glower. "Go out with me."

I choke on a laugh as I scrub a hand over my eyes. "I'm sorry. Man, I am so sorry, Leah. I thought—"

"What did you think?"

I open my eyes again at her soft tone and I find her smiling so gently it takes my breath away.

I swallow. This girl deserves nothing less than the truth. "I thought maybe you'd go out with me if I wasn't so nice. And soothing." I can't help the disgust that fills my voice with that one word and she gives me this adorable wince in response.

With her nose still wrinkled up, she starts to laugh. "I did say that, didn't I?" Now it's her turn to slap a hand over her eyes, which makes me laugh. She peeks at me between her fingers. "I'm an idiot."

"No, *I'm* an idiot," I say. "I've never sounded like such a dick in my entire life. I didn't mean to command you to go out with me, I just really want a chance to take you out. I just really…" I clear my throat as a wave of embarrassment nearly crushes me. "I really want to kiss you."

Her eyes widen. "You do?"

I nod, swallowing hard when her lips part and she goes up on tiptoe. Her hands come to my shoulders to steady herself. "I'd like that."

I groan as I lean in a kiss her. The feel of her lips against mine is sweeter than I could have ever imagined. She gasps when I tilt my head and deepen the kiss slightly, our lips molding and clinging as we explore this new sensation.

"Oh wow," she whispers when I pull back.

I grin down at her. "Wow is right."

We stand there for a long minute grinning at each other like fools. Man, we are such dorks. And I love it.

I reach up to touch her hair because I've been dying to feel her dark locks between my fingers for months now. It's even softer and silkier than it looks. "Does this mean you'll go out with me?" Before she can answer, I hurry on. "I mean, I know you don't have much time left here in Lakeview, so if you can't—"

"I'm staying," she says.

I gape at her for a full second as this registers. "You are?"

Her smile is slow and hesitant. "Does that ruin your plans? If you only want to go out with me because you thought I was leaving—"

I crush her to me before she can finish. Happiness swells so hard and fast it makes my head spin. "You're staying in Lakeview?"

She nods against my shoulder and I hear her light laughter at my response. "I'm staying."

Her hands grip the material of my shirt and for a second we just hold each other tight.

"Since when?" I say when I pull back. "And how? Why? Where did—"

She puts a finger to my lips with a laugh. "I was going to tell you tonight. I wanted to be sure. But first..." She takes a deep breath and my heart tugs at the wariness in her eyes. "I should tell you why I'm not going back."

I nod and we make ourselves comfortable beneath a large oak tree. That's when she tells me a story that makes my heart ache so badly I think it might break. She tells me all about how she was being bullied at her old school, and I don't know whether I want to go to her school and tear those jerks limb from limb or tuck her to my chest and comfort her.

I go with the latter, obviously. She needs my compassion more than my anger.

When she's done with her story, we talk for a long time about why people have to suck so badly, and I tell her the absolute truth. "You are the bravest person I've ever met."

She leans against me as she laughs. "That's sweet of you to say."

"No, I mean it," I say. "I already thought you were amazing for being so sincere and so optimistic, but now..." I shake my head. "Being able to stay so positive when surrounded by such hate...you truly amaze me, Leah."

She leans in to kiss my cheek. "I wanted to tell you all this yesterday, but I lost the nerve." She wrinkles her nose and makes a funny face. "Not so brave now, am I?"

I laugh. "Still brave, just human."

She makes a little humming noise of approval. "Brave but human, I like that."

"I like *you*," I say.

She glances up at me and her eyes glitter with happiness and unshed tears. "I like you too."

I kiss her softly and just when I'm about to draw her into my arms to kiss her even more thoroughly, she pushes back to meet my gaze. "I should tell you that I love that you're nice. I love that you're soothing." She winces. "Even though it was a poor choice of words."

I laugh. "I like that you're nice, too."

She smiles and it makes my heart pound like crazy.

"Can I kiss you again?" I ask.

"I thought you'd never ask," she says with a grin.

As I brush my lips against hers, we both sigh.

Is it dorky that I ask before I kiss her? Maybe. But I don't care because my girl likes a nice guy, and luckily for me, that's exactly what I am.

ABOUT THE AUTHOR

MAGGIE DALLEN IS a big city girl living in Montana. She writes romantic comedies in a range of genres including young adult, historical, contemporary, and fantasy. An unapologetic addict of all things romance, she loves to connect with fellow avid readers. Subscribe to her newsletter at http://eepurl.com/bFEVsL